Richar

Melodies and Madrigals

Mostly from the old English Poets

SALZWASSER
VERLAG

Richard Henry Stoddard

Melodies and Madrigals

Mostly from the old English Poets

1st Edition | ISBN: 978-3-75255-400-7

Place of Publication: Frankfurt am Main, Germany

Year of Publication: 2021

Salzwasser Verlag GmbH, Germany.

Reprint of the original, first published in 1866.

MELODIES AND MADRIGALS;

MOSTLY

FROM THE OLD ENGLISH POETS.

EDITED BY

RICHARD HENRY STODDARD.

"Melodious birds sing madrigals."

Marlowe

NEW YORK:

BUNCE AND HUNTINGTON, PUBLISHERS.

M DCCC LXVI.

PREFACE.

THE object which I had in view while collecting the materials of this volume was, to present the English Poets in their most poetical moods; not as the makers of long, sustained poems, which most of them are not, but as the singers of short, sweet, unpremeditated lyrics. I use the word Lyric rather than Song, because it best describes the selections which follow, and because I take it to be a purer, as it certainly was an earlier, manifestation of the element which underlies the Song. Songs, as we understand them, are of comparatively recent growth. There are no songs, modernly speaking, in SHAKESPEARE and the Elizabethan dramatists, but lyrics in abundance. The difference between these lyrics and our songs is manifest: the one being a simple, unstudied expression of thought, sentiment, or passion; the other its expression according to the mode of the day. The lyrist sang to a tune within him:

("Heard melodies are sweet, but those unheard
Are sweeter; therefore, ye soft pipes, play on!")

The song-writer composes with a strict regard to conventional rhythms and metres, counting his verses on his fingers, and remembering the lessons of his music-teacher. The thought, the sentiment of the former depends upon the whim of the moment; that of the latter, upon the *thesis* which he intends to prove. Reason predominates in the one, Imagination in the other.

The early periods of English Poetry are rich in the Lyrical-element—almost as rich as in the Dramatic, with which it frequently flourished—springing from its excessive vitality, like the myriad wild-flowers which light up the depths of tangled woods. "The little lyrics," says BARRY CORNWALL, "which are scattered, like stars, over the surface of our old dramas, are sometimes minute, trifling, and undefined in their object; but they are often eminently fine; in fact, the finest things of the kind which our language possesses. There is more inspiration, more air and lyrical quality about them, than in songs of ten times their pretension. And this, perhaps, arises from the dramatic faculty of the writers; who, being accustomed, in other things, to shape their verse so as to suit the characters and different purposes of the drama, naturally extend this care to the fashion of the songs themselves. In cases where a writer speaks in his own person, he expends all his egotism upon his lyrics; and requires that a critic should be near to curtail his misdeeds. When he writes as a dramatist, he is, or ought to be, the critic himself. He is not, so to speak, at all implicated in what is going forward in the poem; but deals out the dialogue like an indifferent bystander, seeking only to adjust it to the necessities of the actors. He is above the struggle and turmoil of the battle below, and

'Sees, as from a tower, the end of all.'

It is, in fact, this power of forgetting himself, and of imagining and fashioning characters different from his own, which constitutes the dramatic quality. A man who can set aside his own idiosyncrasy, is half a dramatist."

The lyrics of what we rather loosely call the Elizabethan Poets,—a classification which frequently embraces their successors in the reign of James the First,—are, it seems to me, the finest specimens of poetry, "pure and simple," in the whole range of English Literature. Their chief characteristic is naturalness,—real or apparent, it is not easy, in all cases, to decide which. What we call Art (which is often but another name for artifice), appears never to have crossed the minds of their singers, at least while they were singing; to listen to them is like listening to the song of the lark.

The poets of Charles the First's time—accomplished, courtly gentlemen that they were—delighted in the Lyric, which, however, had begun to lose its early simplicity: it

v

was graceful, it was elegant, but it was studied, mannered, affected.

> "The hour
> Of glory in the grass, of freshness in the flower,"

had passed away. What it was in the reign of Charles the Second, and later, the reader may see for himself, in the specimens of that period which I have given, and which are the best that I could find, indifferent as, I fear, many of them are.

The Eighteenth Century was almost destitute of Lyrics, though it abounded in what were by courtesy called Songs, most of which appear to have been composed by that celebrated Myth, "A Person of Quality," and his, or her, immediate connections—

> "The mob of gentlemen who wrote with ease."

Peace to their ashes! I could not find it in my heart to disturb them, entombed as they are in the ponderous collections of JOHNSON, ANDERSON, and CHALMERS. Barren as the last century was in poetry of a high order, its close witnessed the revival of the Lyrical-element, which may be traced, I think, to two causes,—the publication of Bishop PERCY's "*Reliques of Ancient English Poetry*," and the songs of BURNS—a born poet, if there ever was one, who ruled as supremely over his "scanty plot of ground" as SHAKESPEARE over his Universe.

What the lyrics of the present time are, the reader may be supposed to know. They will not compare with those of the Sixteenth and Seventeenth Centuries, but they are genuine, as far as they go. The best of them, to my thinking, are BARRY CORNWALL's—a venerable name, which must soon pass from amongst us.

The arrangement adopted here is that which should always obtain in works of this nature, viz., the chronological one. The lyrics of each poet are placed in the order in which they were written, so far as I could ascertain it, and the whole in strict succession of time. Where several are taken from one poet, as in the case of SHAKESPEARE and FLETCHER, the date of the earliest determines his place in the century. SHAKESPEARE, for instance, is placed in the year 1592, the date assigned by DYCE to "*Love's Labour's Lost;*" and FLETCHER in 1610, the date of the publication of his "*Faithful Shepherdess.*" Where an author's works were not published until after his death, the lyric, or lyrics, selected therefrom, are, of course, placed before his death. In such cases one can only approximate to correct chronology: certainty is impossible. The student of English Poetry will detect, in most cases, the reasons which have influenced me in assigning the conjectural dates. Had I made the collection for him alone, I would have added annotations of all sorts, which, by-the-way, I could hardly restrain myself from doing. But, working for the general reader, who seldom cares for the laborious trifles of the scholar, however curious they may be, I have let the poets speak for themselves, without note or comment from me. The text is as pure as I could make it. I dare not flatter myself, however, that it is absolutely pure, so much have the old poets been tampered with by those who have edited them, and those who have quoted from them. In the matter of spelling, punctuation, etc., I have conformed to the usage of to-day, not being able to see the sacredness of the old style of typography,—the phonographic spelling of the author, the whims of his printers, and the blunders of the press generally.

R. H. S.

NEW YORK, *November* 1, 1865.

CONTENTS.

TO

EDMUND CLARENCE STEDMAN,

POET, SCHOLAR, GENTLEMAN,

WITH THE LOVE OF HIS FRIEND

R. H. S.

“ The courts of kings hear no such ſtrains
As daily lull the ruſtic swains.”

England's Helicon.

“ I would rather than forty ſhillings I had my book of songs and sonnets here.”

Merry Wives of Windsor.

“ Mark it, Cesario ; it is old and plain :
The spinſters and the knitters in the sun,
And the free maids, that weave their thread with bones,
Do use to chant it ; it is ſilly sooth,
And dallies with the innocence of love,
Like the old age.”

Twelfth Night.

“ They were old-faſhioned poetry, but choicely good, I think much better than the ſtrong lines that are now in faſhion in this critical age.”

Izaak Walton.

MELODIES AND MADRIGALS.

AN EARNEST SUIT

TO HIS UNKIND MISTRESS NOT TO FORSAKE HIM.

[1533?]

I.

AND wilt thou leave me thus?
Say nay, say nay, for ſhame!
To save thee from the blame
Of all my grief and grame.
And wilt thou leave me thus?
Say nay, say nay!

II.

And wilt thou leave me thus?
That hath loved thee so long,
In wealth and woe among?
And is thy heart so ſtrong
As for to leave me thus?
Say nay, say nay!

III.

And wilt thou leave me thus?
That hath given thee my heart,
Never for to depart;
Neither for pain nor smart:
And wilt thou leave me thus?
Say nay, say nay!

IV.

And wilt thou leave me thus?
And have no more pity
Of him that loveth thee?
Alas, thy cruelty!
And wilt thou leave me thus?
Say nay, say nay!

SIR THOMAS WYATT.

A PRAISE OF HIS LOVE,

WHEREIN HE REPROVETH THEM THAT COMPARE THEIR LADIES WITH HIS.

[1535?]

I.

GIVE place, ye lovers, here before
That spent your boasts and brags in vain;
My lady's beauty passeth more
The best of yours, I dare well sayen,
Than doth the sun the candle light,
Or brightest day the darkest night.

II.

And thereto hath a troth as just
As had Penelope the fair;
For what she saith, ye may it trust,
As it by writing sealed were:
And virtues hath she many mo
Than I with pen have skill to show.

III.

I could rehearse, if that I would,
The whole effect of Nature's plaint,
When she had lost the perfect mould
The like to whom she could not paint:
With wringing hands, how she did cry,
And what she said, I know it, aye.

IV.

I know she swore with raging mind,
Her kingdom only set apart,
There was no loss by law of kind
That could have gone so near her heart,
And this was chiefly all her pain:
"She could not make the like again."

V.

Sith Nature thus gave her the praise,
To be the chiefest work she wrought:
In faith, methink, some better ways
On your behalf might well be sought,
Than to compare, as ye have done,
To match the candle with the sun.

HENRY HOWARD, *Earl of Surrey.*

3

A SONNET.

MADE ON ISABELLA MARKHAM, WHEN I FIRST THOUGHT HER FAIR, AS SHE STOOD AT THE PRINCESS'S WINDOW IN GOODLY ATTIRE, AND TALKED TO DIVERS IN THE COURT-YARD.

[1564.]

I.

Whence comes my love? O heart, disclose!
'Twas from cheeks that ſhamed the rose:
From lips that spoil the ruby's praise;
From eyes that mock the diamond's blaze.
Whence comes my woe as freely own;
Ah, me! 'twas from a heart like ſtone.

II.

The bluſhing cheek speaks modeſt mind,
The lips befitting words moſt kind;
The eye does tempt to love's deſire,
And seems to say, 'tis Cupid's fire:
Yet all so fair but speak my moan,
Sith naught doth say the heart of ſtone.

III.

Why thus, my love, so kind bespeak
Sweet lip, sweet eye, sweet bluſhing cheek,
Yet not a heart to save my pain?
O Venus, take thy gifts again!
Make not so fair to cause our moan,
Or make a heart that's like our own.

JOHN HARINGTON.

A DITTY.

[1580?]

I.

MY true love hath my heart, and I have his,
By just exchange one for another given;
I hold his dear, and mine he cannot miss;
There never was a better bargain driven.
My true love hath my heart, and I have his.

II.

His heart in me keeps him and me in one;
My heart in him his thoughts and senses guides:
He loves my heart, for once it was his own;
I cherish his, because in me it bides.
My true love hath my heart, and I have his.

SIR PHILIP SIDNEY.

OF HIS CYNTHIA.

[1580?]

I.

AWAY with these self-loving lads,
Whom Cupid's arrow never glads;
Away, poor souls, that sigh and weep,
In love of them that lie and sleep:
For Cupid is a merry god,
And forceth none to kiss the rod.

II.

Sweet Cupid's ſhafts, like deſtiny,
Do causeless good or ill decree:
Desert is borne out of his bow,
Reward upon his wing doth go.
What fools are they that have not known
That love likes no laws but his own!

III.

My songs they be of Cynthia's praise,
I wear her rings on holy-days;
On every tree I write her name,
And every day I read the same.
Where Honour Cupid's rival is,
There miracles are seen of his.

IV.

If Cynthia crave her ring of me,
I blot her name out of the tree.
If doubt do darken things held dear,
Then well-fare nothing once a year.
For many run, but one muſt win,
Fools only hedge the cuckoo in.

V.

The worth that worthiness ſhould move,
Is love, which is the due of love;
And love as well the ſhepherd can,
As can the mighty nobleman.
Sweet nymph, 'tis true, you worthy be,
Yet without love, naught worth to me.

FULKE GREVILLE, *Lord Brooke.*

SONG.

[1584.]

CUPID and my Campaspe played
At cards for kisses, Cupid paid;
He ſtakes his quiver, bow, and arrows,
His mother's doves, and team of sparrows;
Loses them too; then down he throws
The coral of his lip, the rose
Growing on's cheek, (but none knows how)
With these the cryſtal of his brow,
And then the dimple of his chin;
All these did my Campaspe win.
At laſt he set her both his eyes;
She won, and Cupid blind did rise.
O Love! has ſhe done this to thee?
What ſhall, alas! become of me?

JOHN LYLY.

SONG.

[1584.]

WHAT bird so ſings, yet so does wail?
O 'tis the raviſhed nightingale.
"Jug, jug, jug, jug, terue," ſhe cries,
And ſtill her woes at midnight rise.
Brave prick song! who is't now we hear?
None but the lark so ſhrill and clear;
Now at heaven's gates ſhe claps her wings,
The morn not waking till ſhe ſings.

Hark, hark, with what a pretty throat
Poor robin redbreaſt tunes his note;
Hark, how the jolly cuckoos ſing,
Cuckoo, to welcome in the Spring!
Cuckoo, to welcome in the Spring!

JOHN LYLY.

SONG.

[1592.]

PAN'S Syrinx was a girl indeed,
Though now ſhe's turned into a reed;
From that dear reed Pan's pipe does come,
A pipe that ſtrikes Apollo dumb;
Nor flute, nor lute, nor gittern can
So chant it as the pipe of Pan.
Croſſ-gartered swains and dairy girls,
With faces smug and round as pearls,
When Pan's ſhrill pipe begins to play,
With dancing wear out night and day;
The bagpipe's drone his hum lays by,
When Pan sounds up his minſtrelsy.
His minſtrelsy, O base! This quill,
Which at my mouth with wind I fill,
Puts me in mind, though her I miss,
That ſtill my Syrinx' lips I kiss.

JOHN LYLY. 8

MADRIGAL.

[1588.]

SLEEP, ſleep, mine only jewel,
  Much more thou doſt delight me,
Than my beloved, too cruel,
  That hid her face to spite me.

Thou bring'ſt her home full nigh me,
While ſhe so faſt did fly me.
By thy means I behold those eyes so ſhining,
  Long time absented, that now look appeased;
    Thus is my grief declining:
  Thou in my dreams doſt make deſire well pleased.
Sleep, if thou be like death, as thou art feigned,
A happy life by such a death were gained.

MUSICA TRANSALPINA.

MADRIGAL.

[1588.]

LIKE as from heaven the dew full softly ſhowering,
  Doth fill and so refreſh both fields and closes,
    Filling the parched flowers with sap and savour;
  So while ſhe bathed the violets and roses,
Upon her lovely cheeks so freſhly flowering,
  The Spring renewed his force with her sweet favour.

MUSICA TRANSALPINA.

THE HERDSMAN'S HAPPY LIFE.

[1588.]

WHAT pleasure have great princes,
  More dainty to their choice,
Then herdsmen wild, who, careless,
  In quiet life rejoice,
And fortune's fate not fearing,
Sing sweet in summer morning?

Their dealings, plain and rightful,
  Are void of all deceit;
They never know how spiteful
  It is to kneel and wait,
On favourite presumptuous,
Whose pride is vain and sumptuous.

All day their flocks each tendeth,
  At night they take their reſt,
More quiet than who sendeth
  His ſhip into the Eaſt,
Where gold and pearl are plenty,
But getting very dainty.

For lawyers and their pleading
  They 'ſteem it not a ſtraw;
They think that honeſt meaning
  Is of itself a law;
Where conscience judgeth plainly,
They spend no money vainly

O happy who thus liveth!
Not caring much for gold;
With clothing which sufficeth
To keep him from the cold:
Though poor and plain his diet,
Yet merry it is, and quiet.

BYRD'S SONGS.

ROSALIND'S MADRIGAL.

[1590.]

I.

LOVE in my bosom like a bee
Doth suck his sweet;
Now with his wings he plays with me,
Now with his feet.
Within mine eyes he makes his nest,
His bed amidst my tender breast;
My kisses are his daily feast,
And yet he robs me of my rest.
Ah, wanton, will ye?

II.

And if I sleep, then percheth he
With pretty flight,
And makes his pillow of my knee,
The live-long night.

Strike I my lute, he tunes the ſtring;
He muſic plays if I do ſing;
He lends me every lovely thing:
Yet cruel he my heart doth ſting.
Whiſt, wanton, ſtill ye!

III.

Else I with roses every day
Will whip you hence;
And bind you when you long to play,
For your offence.
I'll ſhut mine eyes to keep you in,
I'll make you faſt it for your ſin,
I'll count your power not worth a pin;
Alas, what hereby ſhall I win,
If he gainsay me?

IV.

What if I beat the wanton boy,
With many a rod?
He will repay me with annoy,
Because a god.
Then ſit thou safely on my knee,
And let thy bower my bosom be:
Lurk in mine eyes, I like of thee.
O Cupid! so thou pity me,
Spare not, but play thee!

Thomas Lodge.

THE SILENT LOVER.

[1590?]

I.

Passions are likened best to floods and streams;
The shallow murmur, but the deep are dumb:
So, when affections yield discourse, it seems
The bottom is but shallow whence they come.
They that are rich in words, in words discover
That they are poor in that which makes a lover.

II.

Wrong not, sweet empress of my heart,
The merit of true passion,
With thinking that he feels no smart,
That sues for no compassion:

III.

Since, if my plaints serve not to approve
The conquest of thy beauty,
It comes not from defect of love,
But from excess of duty:

IV.

For, knowing that I sue to serve
A saint of such perfection,
As all desire, but none deserve,
A place in her affection,

V.

I rather choose to want relief,
Than venture the revealing;
Where glory recommends the grief,
Despair distrusts the healing.

VI.

Thus those desires that aim too high
For any mortal lover,
When reason cannot make them die,
Discretion doth them cover.

VII.

Yet, when discretion doth bereave
The plaints that they should utter,
Then thy discretion may perceive
That silence is a suitor

VIII.

Silence in love bewrays more woe
Than words, though ne'er so witty;
The beggar that is dumb, you know,
May challenge double pity!

IX.

Then wrong not, dearest to my heart,
My true, though secret passion;
He smarteth most that hides his smart,
And sues for no compassion.

SIR WALTER RALEIGH.

PHILLIDA AND CORYDON.

[1591.]

In the merry month of May,
In a morn by break of day,
With a troop of damsels playing,
Forth I yode forsooth a maying.
When anon by a woodſide,
Where that May was in his pride,
I espied all alone
Phillida and Corydon.
Much ado there was, God wot,
He would love, and ſhe would not;
She said, never man was true;
He says, none was false to you.
He said, he had loved her long;
She says, love ſhould have no wrong.
Corydon would kiss her then;
She says, maids muſt kiss no men,
Till they do for good and all:
When ſhe made the ſhepherd call
All the heavens to witness truth,
Never loved a truer youth.
Then with many a pretty oath,
Yea and nay, and faith and troth,
Such as ſilly ſhepherds use,
When they will not love abuse,
Love, that had been long deluded,
Was with kiſſes sweet concluded;
And Phillida, with garlands gay,
Was made the Lady of the May.

NICHOLAS BRETON.

A PASTORAL OF PHILLIS AND CORYDON.

[1600.]

On a hill there grows a flower,
Fair befall the dainty sweet:
By that flower there is a bower
Where the heavenly Muses meet.

In that bower there is a chair,
Fringed all about with gold,
Where doth sit the fairest fair
That ever eye did yet behold.

It is Phillis, fair and bright,
She that is the shepherd's joy:
She that Venus did despite,
And did blind her little boy.

This is she, the wise, the rich,
That the world desires to see:
This is ipsa quæ, *the which*
There is none but only she.

Who would not this face admire?
Who would not this saint adore?
Who would not this sight desire,
Though he thought to see no more?

O fair eyes! yet let me see
One good look, and I am gone.
Look on me, for I am he,
Thy poor silly Corydon.

Thou that art the ſhepherd's queen,
Look upon thy ſilly swain;
By thy comfort have been seen
Dead men brought to life again.

Nicholas Breton.

SONG.

[1591 ?]

What thing is love? for sure love is a thing;
Love is a prick, love is a ſting,
Love is a pretty, pretty thing,
Love is a ſire, love is a coal,
Whose ſlame creeps in at every hole;
And, as myself can beſt devise,
His dwelling is in ladies' eyes,
From whence he ſhoots his dainty darts
Into the luſty gallants' hearts:
And ever ſince was called a god
That Mars and Venus played even and odd.

George Peele.

THE PASSIONATE SHEPHERD TO HIS LOVE.

[1591 ?]

I.

Come live with me, and be my love,
And we will all the pleasures prove,
That valleys, groves, hills, and ſields,
Woods, or ſteepy mountains yields.

II.

And we will sit upon the rocks,
Seeing the shepherds feed their flocks,
By shallow rivers, to whose falls
Melodious birds sing madrigals.

III.

And I will make thee beds of roses,
And a thousand fragrant posies,
A cap of flowers, and a kirtle
Embroidered all with leaves of myrtle.

IV.

A gown made of the finest wool,
Which from our pretty lambs we pull;
Fair-lined slippers for the cold,
With buckles of the purest gold.

V.

A belt of straw and ivy-buds,
With coral clasps and amber studs.
And if these pleasures may thee move,
Come live with me, and be my love.

VI.

The shepherd swains shall dance and sing
For thy delight each May-morning.
If these delights thy mind may move,
Then live with me, and be my love.

CHRISTOPHER MARLOWE.

A DIRGE.

[1592.]

I.

ADIEU; farewell earth's bliss,
This world uncertain is:
Fond are life's luſtful joys,
Death proves them all but toys.
None from his darts can fly:
I am ſick, I muſt die.
Lord, have mercy on us!

II.

Rich men, truſt not in wealth;
Gold cannot buy you health;
Phyſic himself muſt fade;
All things to end are made;
The plague full ſwift goes by:
I am ſick, I muſt die.
Lord, have mercy on us!

III.

Beauty is but a flower,
Which wrinkles will devour:
Brightness falls from the air;
Queens have died young and fair:
Duſt hath closed Helen's eye:
I am ſick, I muſt die.
Lord, have mercy on us!

IV.

Strength stoops unto the grave;
Worms feed on Hector brave.
Swords may not fight with fate:
Earth still holds ope her gate.
Come, come, the hells do cry;
I am sick, I must die.
Lord, have mercy on us!

V.

Wit with his wantonness
Tasteth death's bitterness.
Hell's executioner
Hath no ears for to hear
What vain art can reply;
I am sick, I must die.
Lord, have mercy on us!

VI.

Haste therefore each degree
To welcome destiny:
Heaven is our heritage,
Earth but a player's stage.
Mount we unto the sky;
I am sick, I must die.
Lord, have mercy on us!

THOMAS NASH.

SONG.

[1592.]

SPRING, the sweet Spring, is the year's pleasant King;
Then blooms each thing, then maids dance in a ring;
Cold doth not sting, the pretty birds do sing,
Cuckoo, jug, jug, pu we, to witta woo.

The palm and May make country houses gay,
Lambs frisk and play, the shepherds pipe all day,
And we hear aye birds tune this merry lay,
Cuckoo, jug, jug, pu we, to witta woo.

The fields breathe sweet, the daisies kiss our feet,
Young lovers meet, old wives a sunning sit,
In every street these tunes our ears do greet,
Cuckoo, jug, jug, pu we, to witta woo.
Spring, the sweet Spring.

THOMAS NASH.

PHILOMELA'S ODE

THAT SHE SUNG IN HER ARBOUR.

[1592.]

SITTING by a river's side,
Where a silent stream did glide,
Muse I did of many things,
That the mind in quiet brings.
I 'gan think how some men deem
Gold their god; and some esteem

Honour is the chief content
That to man in life is lent.
And some others do contend,
Quiet none, like to a friend.
Others hold, there is no wealth
Compared to a perfect health.
Some man's mind in quiet ſtands,
When he is lord of many lands:
But I did ſigh, and said all this
Was but a ſhade of perfect bliss;
And in my thoughts I did approve,
Naught so sweet as is true love.
Love 'twixt lovers paſſeth these,
When mouth kiſſeth, and heart 'grees,
With folded arms and lips meeting,
Each soul another sweetly greeting;
For by the breath the soul fleeteth,
And soul with soul in kiſſing meeteth.
If love be so sweet a thing,
That such happy bliss doth bring,
Happy is love's sugared thrall,
But unhappy maidens all,
Who eſteem your virgin bliſſes
Sweeter than a wife's sweet kiſſes.
No such quiet to the mind,
As true love with kiſſes kind:
But if a kiss prove unchaſte,
Then is true love quite disgraced.
Though love be sweet, learn this of me,
No sweet love but honeſty.

ROBERT GREENE.

[1592.]

On a day, (alack the day!)
Love, whose month is ever May,
Spied a blossom, passing fair,
Playing in the wanton air:
Through the velvet leaves the wind,
All unseen, 'gan passage find;
That the lover, sick to death,
Wished himself the heaven's breath.
Air, quoth he, thy cheeks may blow;
Air, would I might triumph so!
But, alack, my hand is sworn
Ne'er to pluck thee from thy thorn:
Vow, alack, for youth unmeet;
Youth, so apt to pluck a sweet.
Do not call it sin in me,
That I am forsworn for thee:
Thou for whom Jove would swear
Juno but an Ethiope were;
And deny himself for Jove,
Turning mortal for thy love.

William Shakespeare.

[1594.]

Over hill, over dale,
Thorough bush, thorough brier,
Over park, over pale,
Thorough flood, thorough fire,

I do wander everywhere,
Swifter than the moon's sphere:
And I serve the fairy queen,
To dew her orbs upon the green.
The cowslips tall her pensioners be;
In their gold coats spots you see,
Those be rubies, fairy favours,
In those freckles live their savours.
I must go seek some dew-drops here,
And hang a pearl in every cowslip's ear.

WILLIAM SHAKESPEARE.

SONG.

[1597.]

TELL me where is fancy bred,
Or in the heart, or in the head?
How begot, how nourished?
Reply, reply.

It is engendered in the eyes,
With gazing fed: and fancy dies
In the cradle where it lies:
Let us all ring fancy's knell;
I'll begin it,—Ding, dong, bell.
Ding, dong, bell.

WILLIAM SHAKESPEARE.

SONG.

[1599.]

UNDER the greenwood tree,
Who loves to lie with me,
And tune his merry note
Unto the sweet bird's throat,
Come hither, come hither, come hither:
Here he ſhall see
No enemy
But winter and rough weather.

Who doth ambition ſhun,
And loves to live i' the sun,
Seeking the food he eats,
And pleased with what he gets,
Come hither, come hither, come hither:
Here he ſhall see
No enemy
But winter and rough weather.

WILLIAM SHAKESPEARE.

SONG.

[1599.]

BLOW, blow, thou winter wind,
Thou art not so unkind
As man's ingratitude;
Thy tooth is not so keen,
Because thou art not seen,
Although thy breath be rude.

Heigh ho! ſing, heigh ho! unto the green holly:
Moſt friendſhip is feigning, moſt loving mere folly:
Then, heigh ho! the holly!
This life is moſt jolly.

Freeze, freeze, thou bitter ſky,
Thou doſt not bite so nigh
As benefits forgot:
Though thou the waters warp,
Thy ſting is not so ſharp
As friend remembered not.
Heigh ho! ſing, heigh ho! unto the green holly:
Moſt friendſhip is feigning, moſt loving mere folly:
Then, heigh ho! the holly!
This life is moſt jolly.

WILLIAM SHAKESPEARE.

SONG.

[1600.]

SIGH no more, ladies, ſigh no more,
Men were deceivers ever;
One foot in sea, and one on ſhore,
To one thing conſtant never:
Then ſigh not so,
But let them go,
And be you blithe and bonny:
Converting all your sounds of woe
Into, Hey nonny, nonny.

Sing no more ditties, ſing no mo
Of dumps so dull and heavy;
The fraud of men was ever so,
Since summer firſt was leavy.
Then ſigh not so,
But let them go,
And be you blithe and bonny:
Converting all your sounds of woe
Into, Hey nonny, nonny.

William Shakespeare.

SONG.

[1601.]

O MISTRESS *mine, where are you roaming?*
O, ſtay and hear; your true love's coming,
That can ſing both high and low:
Trip no further, pretty sweeting;
Journeys end in lovers' meeting,
Every wise man's son doth know.

What is love? 'tis not hereafter;
Present mirth hath present laughter;
What's to come is ſtill unsure:
In delay there lies no plenty;
Then come kiss me, sweet-and-twenty,
Youth's a ſtuff will not endure.

William Shakespeare.

SONG.

[1601.]

Come away, come away, death,
And in sad cypress let me be laid:
Fly away, fly away, breath;
I àm ſlain by a fair cruel maid.
My ſhroud of white, ſtuck all with yew,
O, prepare it!
My part of death, no one so true
Did ſhare it.

Not a flower, not a flower sweet,
On my black coffin let there be ſtrown;
Not a friend, not a friend greet
My poor corpse, where my bones ſhall be thrown:
A thousand thousand ſighs to save,
Lay me, O where
Sad true lover never find my grave,
To weep there!

William Shakespeare.

SONG.

[1603.]

Take, oh! take those lips away,
That so sweetly were forsworn:
And those eyes, the break of day,
Lights that do miſlead the morn:
But my kiſſes bring again,
Bring again,
Seals of love, but sealed in vain,
Sealed in vain.

William Shakespeare.

SONG.

[1609.]

HARK! hark! the lark at heaven's gate sings,
And Phœbus 'gins arise,
His steed to water at those springs
On chaliced flowers that lies:
And winking Mary-buds begin
To ope their golden eyes;
With every thing that pretty bin:
My lady sweet, arise.
Arise, arise.

WILLIAM SHAKESPEARE.

SONG.

[1612.]

FULL fathom five thy father lies:
Of his bones are coral made;
Those are pearls that were his eyes:
Nothing of him that doth fade,
But doth suffer a sea-change
Into something rich and strange.
Sea-nymphs hourly ring his knell:
Hark! now I hear them,—ding, dong, bell.

WILLIAM SHAKESPEARE.

SONG.

[1612.]

Come unto these yellow sands,
And then take hands:
Courtsied when you have, and kissed,
(The wild waves whist)
Foot it featly here and there,
And, sweet sprites, the burden bear.
Hark, hark!
Bowgh, wowgh.
The watch-dogs bark:
Bowgh, wowgh.
Hark, hark! I hear
The strain of strutting chanticleer
Cry, Cock-a-doodle-do.

William Shakespeare.

SONG.

[1612.]

Where the bee sucks, there suck I;
In a cowslip's bell I lie:
There I couch when owls do cry:
On the bat's back I do fly
After summer merrily:
Merrily, merrily, shall I live now,
Under the blossom that hangs on the bough.

William Shakespeare.

SONG.

[1598?]

I.

SWEETEST love, I do not go,
For weariness of thee,
Nor in hope the world can ſhow
A fitter love for me;
But ſince that I
At the laſt muſt part, 'tis beſt
Thus to use myself in jeſt
By feigned deaths to die.

II.

Yeſternight the sun went hence,
And yet is here to-day:
He hath no deſire nor sense,
Nor half so ſhort a way:
Then fear not me,
But believe that I ſhall make
Speedier journeys, ſince I take
More wings and spurs than he.

III.

O how feeble is man's power,
That, if good fortune fall,
Cannot add another hour,
Nor a loſt hour recall!

But come bad chance,
And we join to it our ſtrength,
And we teach it art and length,
Itself o'er us to advance.

IV.

When thou ſigh'ſt thou ſigh'ſt no wind,
But ſigh'ſt my soul away:
When thou weep'ſt, unkindly kind,
My life's blood doth decay:
It cannot be
That thou lov'ſt me, as thou say'ſt,
If in thine my life thou waſte,
That art the beſt of me.

V.

Let not thy divining heart
Forethink me any ill:
Deſtiny may take thy part,
And may thy fears fulfil:
But think that we
Are but turned aſide to ſleep:
They, who one another keep
Alive, ne'er parted be.

JOHN DONNE.

MADRIGAL.

[1598.]

Lady, your words do spite me,
Yet your sweet lips so soft kiss and delight me;
Your deeds my heart surcharged with overjoying,
Your taunts my life destroying;
Since both have force to kill me,
Let kisses sweet, sweet kill me!
Knights fight with swords and lances,
Fight you with smiling glances;
So, like swans of Meander,
My ghost from hence shall wander,
Singing and dying, singing and dying.

Wilbye's Madrigals.

MADRIGAL.

[1598.]

Lady, when I behold the roses sprouting,
Which clad in damask mantles deck the arbours,
And then behold your lips, where sweet love harbours,
My eyes present me with a double doubting;
For viewing both alike, hardly my mind supposes,
Whether the roses be your lips, or your lips the roses.

Wilbye's Madrigals.

MADRIGAL.

[1598.]

LOVE me not for comely grace,
For my pleaſing eye or face;
Not for any outward part,
No, nor for my conſtant heart;
For these may fail, or turn to ill,
And thus we love ſhall sever:
Keep, therefore, a true woman's eye,
And love me ſtill,
Yet know not why;
So haſt thou the same reason ſtill,
To dote upon me ever.

WILBYE'S MADRIGALS.

MADRIGAL.

[1598.]

THERE is a jewel which no Indian mine can buy,
No chemic art can counterfeit;
It makes men rich in greateſt poverty,
Makes water wine, turns wooden cups to gold,
The homely whiſtle to sweet muſic's ſtrain;
Seldom it comes, to few from heaven sent,
That much in little, all in naught—Content.

WILBYE'S MADRIGALS.

MADRIGAL.

[1598.]

CHANGE me, O Heaven! into the ruby ſtone
That on my love's fair locks doth hang in gold,
Yet leave me speech to her to make my moan,
And give me eyes her beauty to behold:
Or if you will not make my fleſh a ſtone,
Make her hard heart seem fleſh, that now is none.

WILBYE'S MADRIGALS.

SPRING-SONG.

[1598.]

I.

IN pride of May
The fields are gay,
The birds do sweetly ſing;
So Nature would
That all things ſhould
With joy begin the Spring.

II.

Then, lady dear,
Do you appear,
In beauty like the Spring;
I dare well say,
The birds that day,
More cheerfully will ſing.

WEELKES'S BALLADS AND MADRIGALS.

AN ODE.

[1598.]

As it fell upon a day,
In the merry month of May,
Sitting in a pleasant ſhade,
Which a grove of myrtles made,
Beaſts did leap, and birds did ſing,
Trees did grow, and plants did spring,
Every thing did baniſh moan,
Save the nightingale alone:
She, poor bird, as all forlorn,
Leaned her breaſt up-till a thorn,
And there sang the dolefull'ſt ditty,
That to hear it was great pity.
Fie, fie, fie, now ſhe would cry,
Teru, teru, by and by;
That to hear her so complain,
Scarce I could from tears refrain;
For her griefs, so lively ſhown,
Made me think upon mine own.
Ah! thought I, thou mourn'ſt in vain;
None take pity on thy pain;
Senseless trees, they cannot hear thee,
Ruthless bears, they will not cheer thee;
King Pandion, he is dead;
All thy friends are lapped in lead;
All thy fellow-birds do ſing,
Careless of thy sorrowing.
Even so, poor bird, like thee,
None alive will pity me.

Whilst as fickle Fortune smiled,
Thou and I were both beguiled,
Every one that flatters thee,
Is no friend of misery.
Words are easy, like the wind;
Faithful friends are hard to find.
Every man will be thy friend,
When thou hast wherewith to spend:
But if store of crowns be scant,
No man will supply thy want.
If that one be prodigal,
Bountiful they will him call;
And with such-like flattering,
"Pity but he were a king."
If he be addict to vice,
Quickly him they will entice:
If to women he be bent,
They have him at commandement;
But if Fortune once do frown,
Then farewell his great renown:
They that fawned on him before,
Use his company no more.
He that is thy friend indeed,
He will help thee in thy need;
If thou sorrow, he will weep,
If thou wake, he cannot sleep:
Thus of every grief in heart
He with thee doth bear a part.
These are certain signs to know
Faithful friend from flattering foe.

Richard Barnefield.

SONG.

[1599.]

I.

ART thou poor, yet hast thou golden slumbers?
O sweet content!
Art thou rich, yet is thy mind perplexed?
O punishment!
Dost thou laugh to see how fools are vexed
To add to golden numbers, golden numbers?
O sweet content! O sweet, O sweet content!
Work apace, apace, apace, apace,
Honest labour bears a lovely face;
Then hey nonny, nonny, hey nonny, nonny!

II.

Canst drink the waters of the crisped spring?
O sweet content!
Swimm'st thou in wealth, yet sink'st in thine own tears?
O punishment!
Then he that patiently want's burden bears
No burden bears, but is a king, a king!
O sweet content! O sweet, O sweet content!
Work apace, apace, apace, apace,
Honest labour bears a lovely face:
Then hey nonny, nonny, hey nonny, nonny!

THOMAS DEKKER.

TO THE SPRING.

[1599.]

I.

EARTH now is green, and heaven is blue,
Lively Spring, which makes all new,
Jolly Spring doth enter;
Sweet young sunbeams do subdue
Angry, aged Winter.

II.

Blasts are mild, and seas are calm,
Every meadow flows with balm,
The Earth wears all her riches:
Harmonious birds sing such a psalm
As ear and heart bewitches.

III.

Reserve, sweet Spring, this nymph of ours,
Eternal garlands of thy flowers,
Green garlands, never wasting;
In her shall last our State's fair spring,
Now and forever flourishing,
As long as heaven is lasting.

SIR JOHN DAVIES.

THE COY MAIDEN'S CONSENT.

[1599.]

I.

O STAY, sweet love, see here the place of sporting,
These gentle flowers smile sweetly to invite us;
And chirping birds are hitherwards resorting,
Warbling sweet notes only to delight us.
Then stay, dear love, for though thou run from me,
Run ne'er so fast, yet I will follow thee.

II.

I thought, my love, that I should overtake you;
Sweet heart, sit down under this shadowed tree,
And I will promise never to forsake you,
So you will grant to me a lover's fee.
Whereat she smiled, and kindly to me said,
I never meant to live and die a maid.

FARMER'S ENGLISH MADRIGALS.

THE FLIGHT OF PHILLIS.

[1599.]

FAIR Phillis I saw sitting all alone,
Feeding her flock near to the mountain side;
The shepherds knew not whither she was gone,
But after her her lover, Amyntas, hied.
He wandered up and down whilst she was missing:
When he found her, then they fell a-kissing.

FARMER'S ENGLISH MADRIGALS.

DAMELUS' SONG TO HIS DIAPHENIA.

[1600.]

I.

DIAPHENIA, like the daffadowndilly,
White as the sun, fair as the lily,
Heigh ho, how I do love thee!
I do love thee as my lambs
Are beloved of their dams;
How blest were I if thou wouldst prove me!

II.

Diaphenia, like the spreading roses,
That in thy sweets all sweets encloses,
Fair sweet, how I do love thee!
I do love thee as each flower
Loves the sun's life-giving power;
For dead, thy breath to life might move me.

III.

Diaphenia, like to all things blessed,
When all thy praises are expressed,
Dear joy, how I do love thee!
As the birds do love the Spring,
Or the bees their careful king;
Then in requite, sweet virgin, love me!

HENRY CONSTABLE.

THE NYMPHS,

MEETING THEIR MAY QUEEN, ENTERTAIN HER WITH THIS DITTY.

[1600.]

I.

WITH fragrant flowers we strew the way,
And make this our chief holy-day.
For though this clime were blest of yore,
Yet was it never proud before.
O beauteous queen of second Troy,
Accept of our unfeigned joy.

II.

Now th' air is sweeter than sweet balm,
And satyrs dance about the palm;
Now Earth with verdure newly dight
Gives perfect signs of her delight.
O beauteous queen of second Troy,
Accept of our unfeigned joy.

III.

Now birds record new harmony,
And trees do whistle melody;
Now every thing that Nature breeds,
Doth clad itself in pleasant weeds.
O beauteous queen of second Troy,
Accept of our unfeigned joy.

THOMAS WATSON.

FALSE DORUS.

[1600.]

In dew of roses steeping
Her lovely cheeks, Lycoris sat weeping:
Ah, Dorus false! thou hast my heart bereft me,
And now, unkind, hast left me.
Hear, alas! O hear me!
Ay me! ay me!
Cannot my beauty move thee?
Pity, then, pity me,
Because I love thee.
Ay me! thou scorn'st the more I pray thee,
And this thou dost to slay me.
Ah, do, then, do, kill me and vaunt thee;
Yet my ghost still shall haunt thee.

Morley's Madrigals.

INVOCATION TO NIGHT.

[1600.]

I.

Come, you heavy states of night,
Do my father's spirit right.
Soundings baleful let me borrow,
Burthening my song with sorrow.
Come, sorrow, come; her eyes that sings
By thee are turned into springs.

II.

Come, you virgins of the night,
That in dirges sad delight,
Quire my anthems; I do borrow
Gold nor pearl, but sounds of sorrow.
Come, sorrow, come; her eyes that sings
By thee are turned into springs.

DOWLAND'S BOOK OF SONGS.

TO CYNTHIA.

[1600.]

I.

MY thoughts are winged with hopes, my hopes with love,
Mount, love, unto the moon in clearest night,
And say, as she doth in the heavens move,
In earth so wanes and waxes my delight.
And whisper this, but softly in her ears,
Hope oft doth hang the head, and trust shed tears.

II.

And you, my thoughts, that some mistrust do carry,
If for mistrust my mistress you do blame,
Say, though you alter, yet you do not vary,
As she doth change, and yet remain the same.
Distrust doth enter hearts, but not infect,
And love is sweetest seasoned with suspect.

III.

If ſhe for this with clouds do maſk her eyes,
And make the heavens dark with her disdain,
With windy ſighs disperse them in the ſkies,
Or with thy tears diſſolve them into rain.
Thoughts, hopes, and love return to me no more,
Till Cynthia ſhine as ſhe hath done before.

DOWLAND'S BOOK OF SONGS.

HIS LADY'S GRIEF.

[1600.]

I.

I SAW my lady weep,
And sorrow proud to be advanced so
In those fair eyes, where all perfections keep.
Her face was full of woe,
But such a woe, believe me, as wins more hearts,
Then mirth can do with her enticing parts.

II.

Sorrow was there made fair,
And paſſion wise, tears a delightful thing,
Silence beyond all speech a wisdom rare;
She made her ſighs to ſing,
And all things with so sweet a sadness move,
As made my heart at once both grieve and love.

III.

O! fairer than aught else
The world can ſhow, leave off in time to grieve;
Enough, enough, your joyful look excels:
Tears kill the heart, believe.
O, ſtrive not to be excellent in woe,
Which only breeds your beauties' overthrow.

DOWLAND'S BOOK OF SONGS.

MADRIGAL.

[1600.]

I.

WHY are you, ladies, ſtaying,
And your lords gone a-Maying:
Run apace and meet them,
And with your garlands greet them;
'Twere pity they ſhould miss you,
For they will sweetly kiss you.

II.

Hark, hark, I hear the dancing,
And a nimble morris prancing;
The bagpipe and the morris bells,
That they are not far hence us tells:
Come, let us all go thither,
And dance like friends together.

WEELKES'S MADRIGALS.

MADRIGAL.

[1600.]

Cold winter's ice is fled and gone,
And summer hangs on every tree;
The redbreast peeps amidst the throng
Of wood-born birds that wanton be:
Each one forgets what they have been,
And so doth Phillis, summer's queen.

Weelkes's Madrigals.

OF CORINNA'S SINGING.

[1602.]

I.

When to her lute Corinna sings,
Her voice revives the leaden strings,
And doth in highest notes appear,
As any challenged echo clear:
But when she doth of mourning speak,
Even with her sighs the strings do break.

II.

And as her lute doth live or die,
Led by her passions, so must I:
For when of pleasure she doth sing,
My thoughts enjoy a sudden spring:
But if she do of sorrow speak,
Even from my heart the strings do break.

Thomas Campion.

MADRIGAL.

[1602.]

I.

Give Beauty all her right,
She's not to one form tied;
Each ſhape yields fair delight,
Where her perfections bide:
Helen, I grant, might pleaſing be,
And Rosamond was as sweet as ſhe.

II.

Some the quick eye commends,
Some swelling lips, and red;
Pale looks have many friends,
Through sacred sweetness bred.
Meadows have flowers that pleasure move,
Though roses are the flowers of love.

III.

True Beauty is not bound
To one unmoved clime:
She viſits every ground,
And favours every time.
Let the old loves with mine compare,
My sovereign is as sweet and fair.

Thomas Campion.

A SONG.

IN PRAISE OF A BEGGAR'S LIFE.

[1602.]

Bright ſhines the sun, play, beggars, play,
Here's scraps enough to serve to-day.

What noise of viols is so sweet
As when our merry clappers ring?
What mirth doth want where beggars meet?
A beggar's life is for a king:
Eat, drink, and play; ſleep when we liſt,
Go where we will, so ſtocks be miſſed.
Bright ſhines the sun, play, beggars, play,
Here's scraps enough to serve to-day.

The world is ours, and ours alone,
For we alone have worlds at will:
We purchase not, 'tis all our own,
Both fields and ſtreets we beggars fill:
Nor care to get, nor fear to keep,
Did ever break a beggar's ſleep.
Bright ſhines the sun, play, beggars, play,
Here's scraps enough to serve to-day.

A hundred head of black and white
Upon our gowns securely feed;
If any dares his maſter bite,
He dies therefor, as sure as creed.

Thus beggars lord it as they please;
And only beggars live at ease.
Bright ſhines the sun, play, beggars, play,
Here's scraps enough to serve to-day.

DAVISON'S POETICAL RHAPSODY.

ODE.

PETITION TO HAVE HER LEAVE TO DIE.

[1602.]

WHEN will the fountain of my tears be dry?
When will my ſighs be spent?
When will deſire agree to let me die?
When will thy heart relent?
It is not for my life I plead,
Since death the way to reſt doth lead;
But ſtay for thy consent,
Leſt thou be discontent.

For if myself without thy leave I kill,
My ghoſt will never reſt;
So hath it sworn to work thine only will,
And holds that ever beſt.
For ſince it only lives by thee,
Good reason thou the ruler be:
Then give me leave to die,
And ſhow thy power thereby.

DAVISON'S POETICAL RHAPSODY.

MADRIGAL.

[1602.]

My love in her attire doth ſhow her wit,
It doth so well become her;
For every season ſhe hath dreſſings fit,
For winter, spring, and summer.
No beauty ſhe doth miss,
When all her robes are on:
For Beauty's self ſhe is
When all her robes are gone.

DÁVISON'S POETICAL RHAPSODY.

MADRIGAL.

[1604.]

HOLD out, my heart, with joy's delights accloyed;
Hold out, my heart, and ſhow it,
That all the world may know it,
What sweet content thou lately haſt enjoyed.
She that, Come, dear, would say,
Then laugh, and smile, and run away,
And if I ſtayed her would cry, Nay,
Fie, for ſhame, fie!
My true love not regarding,
Hath given me at length his full rewarding:

So that unless I tell
The joys that overfill me,
My joys, kept in full well,
I know will kill me.

WEELKES'S MADRIGALS.

THERE IS A GARDEN IN HER FACE.

[1606.]

THERE is a garden in her face,
Where roses and white lilies blow;
A heavenly paradise is that place,
Wherein all pleasant fruits do grow:
There cherries grow that none may buy,
Till cherry-ripe themselves do cry.

Those cherries fairly do enclose
Of orient pearl a double row,
Which when her lovely laughter ſhows,
They look like rose-buds filled with snow:
Yet them nor peer nor prince may buy,
Till cherry-ripe themselves do cry.

Her eyes like angels watch them ſtill;
Her brows like bended bows do ſtand,
Threatening with piercing frowns to kill
All that approach with eye or hand
Those sacred cherries to come nigh,
Till cherry-ripe themselves do cry.

ALLISON'S HOUR'S RECREATION IN MUSIC.

SONG.

[1606?]

I DO confess thou'rt smooth and fair,
And I might have gone near to love thee,
Had I not found the ſlighteſt prayer
That lips could speak had power to move thee:
But I can let thee now alone,
As worthy to be loved by none.

I do confess thou'rt sweet, yet find
Thee such an unthrift of thy sweets,
Thy favours are but like the wind,
That kiſſes every thing it meets;
And ſince thou canſt with more than one,
Thou'rt worthy to be kiſſed by none.

The morning rose, that untouched ſtands,
Armed with her briers, how sweetly smells!
But plucked and ſtrained through ruder hands,
Her sweets no longer with her dwells;
But scent and beauty both are gone,
And leaves fall from her one by one.

Such fate, ere long, will thee betide,
When thou haſt handled been awhile,
Like sere flowers to be thrown aſide:
And I will ſigh, while some will smile,
To see thy love for more than one
Hath brought thee to be loved by none.

SIR ROBERT AYTON.

MADRIGAL.

[1606.]

WHITHER so fast? Ah, see the kindly flowers
Perfume the air, and all to make thee stay:
The climbing woodbine, clipping all these bowers,
Clips thee likewise, for fear thou pass away:
Fortune, our friend, our foe, will not gainsay:
Stay but awhile, Phœbe no tell-tale is:
She her Endymion—I'll my Phœbe kiss.

BATESON'S MADRIGALS.

SONG.

[1607.]

I.

PACK clouds away, and welcome day,
With night we banish sorrow;
Sweet air, blow soft, mount, lark, aloft,
To give my love good-morrow.
Wings from the wind to please her mind,
Notes from the lark I'll borrow;
Bird, prune thy wing, nightingale, sing,
To give my love good-morrow.
To give my love good-morrow,
Notes from them both I'll borrow.

II.

Wake from thy neſt, robin redbreaſt,
Sing, birds, in every furrow;
And from each hill let muſic ſhrill
Give my fair love good-morrow.
Blackbird, and thruſh, in every buſh,
Stare, linnet, and cock-sparrow;
You pretty elves, amongſt yourselves,
Sing my fair love good-morrow.
To give my love good-morrow,
Sing, birds, in every furrow.

THOMAS HEYWOOD.

MADRIGAL.

[1608.]

UPON *a hill the bonny boy,*
Sweet Thirſis, sweetly played,
And called his lambs their maſter's joy;
And more he would have said,
But love that gives the lover's wings,
Withdrew his mind from other things.

His pipe and he could not agree,
For Milla was his note:
The ſilly pipe could never get
This lovely name by rote:
With that they both fell on a sound,
He fell aſleep, his pipe to ground.

WEELKES'S AIRS.

SONG.

[1609.]

STILL to be neat, ſtill to be dreſt,
As you were going to a feaſt;
Still to be powdered, ſtill perfumed;
Lady, it is to be presumed,
Though art's hid causes are not found,
All is not sweet, all is not sound.

Give me a look, give me a face
That makes ſimplicity a grace;
Robes loosely flowing, hair as free:
Such sweet neglect more taketh me
Than all the adulteries of art;
They ſtrike mine eyes, but not my heart.

BEN JONSON.

TO CELIA.

[1616.]

DRINK to me only with thine eyes,
And I will pledge with mine;
Or leave a kiss but in the cup,
And I'll not look for wine.
The thirſt that from the soul doth rise,
Doth aſk a drink divine;
But might I of Jove's nectar sup,
I would not change for thine.

I sent thee late a rosy wreath,
Not so much honouring thee,
As giving it a hope that there
It could not withered be.
But thou thereon didst only breathe,
And sent'st it back to me:
Since when it grows, and smells, I swear,
Not of itself, but thee.

BEN JONSON.

TO CELIA.

[1616.]

Kiss me, sweet; the wary lover
Can your favours keep, and cover,
When the common courting jay
All your bounties will betray.
Kiss again! no creature comes;
Kiss, and score up wealthy sums
On my lips, thus hardly sundered,
While you breathe. First give a hundred,
Then a thousand, then another
Hundred, then unto the other
Add a thousand, and so more;
Till you equal with the store,
All the grass that Rumney yields,
Or the sands in Chelsea fields,

Or the drops in ſilver Thames,
Or the ſtars that gild his ſtreams,
In the ſilent summer-nights,
When youths ply their ſtolen delights;
That the curious may not know
How to tell 'em as they flow;
And the envious, when they find
What their number is, be pined.

BEN JONSON.

THE TRIUMPH OF CHARIS.

[1616?]

SEE the chariot at hand here of Love,
Wherein my lady rideth!
Each that draws is a swan or a dove,
And well the car Love guideth.
As ſhe goes, all hearts do duty
Unto her beauty;
And, enamoured, do wiſh, so they might
But enjoy such a ſight,
That they ſtill were to run by her ſide,
Through swords, through seas, whither ſhe would ride.

Do but look on her eyes, they do light
All that Love's world compriseth!
Do but look on her hair, it is bright
As Love's ſtar when it riseth!
Do but mark, her forehead's smoother
Than words that soothe her!

And from her arched brows, such a grace
Sheds itself through the face,
As alone there triumphs to the life
All the gain, all the good, of the elements' ſtrife.

Have you seen but a bright lily grow,
Before rude hands have touched it?
Have you marked but the fall o' the snow,
Before the soil hath smutched it?
Have you felt the wool of beaver?
Or swan's down ever?
Or have smelt o' the bud o' the brier?
Or the nard in the fire?
Or have taſted the bag of the bee?
O so white! O so soft! O so sweet is ſhe!

BEN JONSON.

THE WOOING SONG OF PANGLORY.

[1610.]

LOVE is the bloſſom where there blows
Every thing that lives or grows;
Love doth make the heavens to move,
And the sun doth burn in love:
Love the ſtrong and weak doth yoke,
And makes the ivy climb the oak,
Under whose ſhadows lions wild,
Softened by love, grow tame and mild.
Love no medicine can appease;
He burns the fiſhes in the seas:

Not all the ſkill his wounds can ſtanch,
Not all the sea his fire can quench.
Love did make the bloody spear
Once a leavy coat to wear,
While in his leaves there ſhrouded lay
Sweet birds, for love that ſing and play;
And of all Love's joyful ſlame
I the bud and bloſſom am.
Only bend thy knee to me,
Thy wooing ſhall thy winning be.

See, see the flowers that below
Now as freſh as morning blow,
And of all, the virgin rose,
That as bright Aurora ſhows;
How they all unleaved die,
Loſing their virginity:
Like unto a summer-ſhade,
But now born, and now they fade.
Every thing doth pass away;
There is danger in delay.
Come, come gather, then, the rose;
Gather it, or it you lose.
All the sand of Tagus' ſhore
In my bosom caſts his ore:
All the valleys' swimming corn
To my house is yearly borne:
Every grape of every vine
Is gladly bruised to make me wine;
While ten thousand kings, as proud
To carry up my train, have bowed,

And a world of ladies send me
In my chambers to attend me:
All the ſtars in heaven that ſhine,
And ten thousand more, are mine.
Only bend thy knee to me,
Thy wooing ſhall thy winning be.

GILES FLETCHER.

SONG.

[1610.]

Do not fear to put thy feet
Naked in the river, sweet;
Think not leech, or newt, or toad,
Will bite thy foot, when thou haſt trod;
Nor let the water riſing high,
As thou wad'ſt in, make thee cry,
And sob; but ever live with me,
And not a wave ſhall trouble thee.

JOHN FLETCHER.

SONG.

[1617?]

WEEP no more, nor ſigh, nor groan,
Sorrow calls no time that's gone;
Violets plucked, the sweeteſt rain
Makes not freſh, nor grow again.

Trim thy locks, look cheerfully;
Fate's hidden ends eyes cannot see;
Joys as winged dreams fly fast,
Why should sadness longer last?
Grief is but a wound to woe;
Gentlest fair, mourn, mourn no mo.

JOHN FLETCHER.

SONG.

[1624?]

'TIS late and cold; stir up the fire;
Sit close, and draw the table nigher;
Be merry, and drink wine that's old,
A hearty medicine 'gainst a cold:
Your beds of wanton down the best,
Where you shall tumble to your rest;
I could wish you wenches too,
But I am dead, and cannot do.
Call for the best the house may ring,
Sack, white, and claret, let them bring,
And drink apace, while breath you have;
You'll find but cold drink in the grave:
Plover, partridge for your dinner,
And a capon for the sinner,
You shall find ready when you're up,
And your horse shall have his sup:
Welcome, welcome, shall fly round,
And I shall smile, though under ground.

JOHN FLETCHER.

SONG.

[1624?]

Take, oh! take those lips away,
That so sweetly were forsworn,
And those eyes, like break of day,
Lights that do mislead the morn!
But my kisses bring again,
Seals of love, though sealed in vain.

Hide, oh! hide those hills of snow,
Which thy frozen bosom bears,
On whose tops the pinks that grow
Are yet of those that April wears!
But first set my poor heart free,
Bound in those icy chains by thee.

John Fletcher.

SONG.

[1624?]

Drink to-day, and drown all sorrow,
You shall perhaps not do it to-morrow:
Best, while you have it, use your breath;
There is no drinking after death.

Wine works the heart up, wakes the wit,
There is no cure 'gainst age but it;
It helps the head-ache, cough, and phthisic,
And is for all diseases physic.

Then let us swill, boys, for our health;
Who drinks well loves the commonwealth.
And he that will to bed go sober,
Falls with the leaf, ſtill in October.

JOHN FLETCHER.

SONG.

[1624?]

HENCE, all you vain delights,
As ſhort as are the nights
Wherein you spend your folly!
There's naught in this life sweet,
If men were wise to see't,
But only melancholy!
O, sweeteſt melancholy!
Welcome, folded arms, and fixed eyes,
A ſigh, that, piercing, mortifies;
A look that's faſtened to the ground,
A tongue chained up without a sound!
Fountain heads, and pathless groves,
Places which pale Paſſion loves!
Moonlight walks, when all the fowls
Are warmly housed, save bats and owls!
A midnight bell, a parting groan,
These are the sounds we feed upon;
Then ſtretch our bones in a ſtill gloomy valley,
Nothing's so dainty sweet as lovely melancholy.

JOHN FLETCHER.

MADRIGAL.

[1612.]

HAVE I found her? O rich finding!
Goddess-like for to behold;
Her fair tresses seemly binding
In a chain of pearl and gold:
Chain me, chain me, oh most fair,
Chain me to thee with that hair!

PILKINGTON'S MADRIGALS.

[1612.]

SHALL I, wasting in despair,
Die, because a woman's fair?
Or make pale my cheeks with care,
'Cause another's rosy are?
Be she fairer than the day,
Or the flowery meads in May,
If she be not so to me,
What care I how fair she be?

Shall my foolish heart be pined,
'Cause I see a woman kind,
Or a well-disposed nature,
Joined with a lovely feature?
Be she meeker, kinder, than
Turtle-dove or pelican,

If ſhe be not so to me,
What care I how kind ſhe be?

Shall a woman's virtues move
Me to periſh for her love?
Or her well-deserving known,
Make me quite forget mine own?
Be ſhe with that goodness bleſt,
Which may gain her name of beſt,
If ſhe be not such to me,
What care I how good ſhe be?

'Cause her fortune seems too high,
Shall I play the fool and die?
Those that bear a noble mind,
Where they want of riches find,
Think what with them they would do,
That without them dare to woo:
And unless that mind I see,
What care I how great ſhe be?

Great, or good, or kind, or fair,
I will ne'er the more despair.
If ſhe love me, this believe,
I will die ere ſhe ſhall grieve:
If ſhe ſlight me, when I woo,
I can scorn, and let her go.
For if ſhe be not for me,
What care I for whom ſhe be?

George Wither.

[1612.]

CALL for the robin redbreaſt and the wren,
Since o'er ſhady groves they hover,
And with leaves and flowers do cover
The friendless bodies of unburied men.
Call unto his funeral dole
The ant, the field-mouse, and the mole,
To rear him hillocks that ſhall keep him warm,
And (when gay tombs are robbed) ſuſtain no harm:
But keep the wolf far thence, that's foe to men,
For with his nails he'll dig them up again.

JOHN WEBSTER

[1616?]

HARK, now every thing is ſtill;
The screech-owl and the whiſtler ſhrill
Call upon our dame aloud,
And bid her quickly don her ſhroud!
Much you had of land and rent;
Your length in clay's now competent:
A long war diſturbed your mind;
Here your perfect peace is ſigned.
Of what is't fools make such vain keeping?
Sin their conception, their birth weeping,
Their life a general miſt of error,
Their death a hideous ſtorm of terror.

Strew your hair with powders sweet,
Don clean linen, bathe your feet,
And (the foul fiend more to check)
A crucifix let bless your neck:
'Tis now full tide 'tween night and day,
End your groan, and come away.

JOHN WEBSTER.

[1623.]

ALL the flowers of the Spring
Meet to perfume our burying:
These have but their growing prime,
And man does flourish but his time.
Survey our progress from our birth;
We are set, we grow, we turn to earth.
Courts adieu, and all delights,
All bewitching appetites!
Sweetest breath, and clearest eye,
Like perfumes, go out and die;
And consequently this is done
As shadows wait upon the sun.
Vain the ambition of kings,
Who seek by trophies and dead things
To leave a living name behind,
And weave but nets to catch the wind.

JOHN WEBSTER.

MADRIGAL.

[1613?]

O SAY, dear life, when ſhall those twin-born berries,
So lovely ripe, by my rude lips be taſted?
Shall I not pluck—sweet, say not nay!—those cherries?
O let them not with summer's heat be blaſted!
Nature, thou know'ſt, beſtowed them free on thee;
Then be thou kind, beſtow them free on me.

WARD'S MADRIGALS.

THE CHARACTER OF A HAPPY LIFE.

[1614.]

How happy is he born and taught,
That serveth not another's will:
Whose armour is his honeſt thought,
And ſimple truth his utmoſt ſkill

Whose paſſions not his maſters are;
Whose soul is ſtill prepared for death,
Untied unto the world by care
Of public fame, or private breath.

Who envies none that chance doth raise,
Nor vice; who never underſtood
How deepeſt wounds are given by praise;
Nor rules of State, but rules of good.

Who hath his life from rumours freed;
Whose conscience is his ſtrong retreat;
Whose ſtate can neither flatterers feed,
Nor ruin make oppreſſors great.

Who GOD *doth late and early pray*
More of his Grace than gifts to lend;
And entertains the harmless day
With a religious book, or friend.

This man is freed from servile bands
Of hope to rise, or fear to fall:
Lord of himself, though not of lands,
And having nothing, yet hath all.

SIR HENRY WOTTON.

ON HIS MISTRESS, THE QUEEN OF BOHEMIA.

[1620.]

YOU meaner beauties of the night,
That poorly satisfy our eyes,
More by your number than your light,
You common people of the ſkies,
What are you when the sun ſhall rise?

You curious chanters of the wood,
That warble forth Dame Nature's lays,
Thinking your paſſions underſtood
By your weak accents, what's your praise,
When Philomel her voice ſhall raise?

You violets that first appear,
By your pure purple mantles known,
Like the proud virgins of the year,
As if the Spring were all your own,
What are you when the rose is blown?

So, when my mistress shall be seen,
In form, and beauty of her mind,
By virtue first, then choice, a queen,
Tell me, if she were not designed
Th' eclipse and glory of her kind?

SIR HENRY WOTTON.

THE INDIFFERENT.

[1615?]

I.

NEVER more will I protest
To love a woman, but in jest:
For as they cannot be true,
So to give each man his due,
When the wooing fit is past,
Their affection cannot last.

II.

Therefore if I chance to meet
With a mistress, fair and sweet,
She my service shall obtain,
Loving her for love again:

This much liberty I crave,
Not to be a constant slave.

III.

But when we have tried each other,
If she better like another,
Let her quickly change for me,
Then to change am I as free.
He or she that loves too long,
Sell their freedom for a song.

FRANCIS BEAUMONT.

MADRIGAL.

[1616.]

I FEAR *not henceforth death,*
Sith after this departure yet I breathe;
Let rocks, and seas, and wind,
Their highest treasons show:
Let sky and earth combined
Strive, if they can, to end my life and woe;
Sith grief cannot, me nothing can o'erthrow:
Or if that aught can cause my fatal lot,
It will be when I hear I am forgot.

WILLIAM DRUMMOND.

A KISS.

[1616.]

HARK, happy lovers, hark,
This firſt and laſt of joys,
This sweetener of annoys,
This nectar of the gods
Ye call a kiss, is with itself at odds;
And half so sweet is not
In equal measure got
At light of sun, as it is in the dark:
Hark, happy lovers, hark.

WILLIAM DRUMMOND.

DESIRED DEATH.

[1631?]

DEAR life, while I do touch
These coral ports of bliss,
Which ſtill themselves do kiss,
And sweetly me invite to do as much,
All panting in my lips
My heart my sense doth leave,
No sense my senses have,
And inward powers do find a ſtrange eclipse;
This death so heavenly well
Doth so me please, that I
Would never longer seek in sense to dwell,
If that even thus I only could but die.

WILLIAM DRUMMOND.

TO SLEEP.

[1631?]

HOW comes it, Sleep, that thou
Even kiſſes me affords
Of her, dear her, so far who's absent now?
How did I hear those words,
Which rocks might move, and move the pines to bow?
Ay me, before half day
Why didſt thou ſteal away?
Return, I thine forever will remain,
If thou wilt bring with thee that gueſt again.

WILLIAM DRUMMOND.

[1616.]

SHALL I tell you whom I love?
Hearken then awhile to me;
And if such a woman move,
As I now ſhall verſify,
Be aſſured 'tis ſhe, or none,
That I love, and love alone.

Nature did her so much right,
As ſhe scorns the help of art;
In as many virtues dight
As e'er yet embraced a heart:
So much good, so truly tried,
Some for less were deified.

Wit ſhe hath, without deſire
To make known how much ſhe hath;
And her anger flames no higher
Than may fitly sweeten wrath.
Full of pity as may be,
Though, perhaps, not so for me.

Reason maſters every sense,
And her virtues grace her birth;
Lovely as all excellence,
Modeſt in her moſt of mirth:
Likelihood enough to prove
Only worth could kindle love.

Such ſhe is: and if you know
Such a one as I have sung;
Be ſhe brown, or fair, or so,
That ſhe be but some-while young;
Be aſſured 'tis ſhe, or none,
That I love, and love alone.

WILLIAM BROWNE.

SONG.

[1620?]

STEER, hither ſteer, your winged pines,
All beaten mariners;
Here lie Love's undiscovered mines,
A prey to paſſengers:
Perfumes far sweeter than the beſt
Which make the phœnix' urn and neſt.

Fear not your ſhips,
Nor any to oppose you, save our lips:
But come on ſhore,
Where no joy dies till Love hath gotten more.

For swelling waves, our panting breaſts,
Where never ſtorms arise,
Exchange, and be awhile our gueſts;
For ſtars, gaze on our eyes.
The compass Love ſhall hourly ſing,
And, as he goes about the ring,
We will not miss
To tell each point he nameth with a kiss.
Then come on ſhore,
Where no joy dies till Love hath gotten more.

WILLIAM BROWNE.

SONG.

[1617?]

I.

LOVE is a ſickness full of woes,
All remedies refuſing;
A plant that with moſt cutting grows,
Moſt barren with beſt uſing.
Why so?
More we enjoy it, more it dies;
If not enjoyed, it ſighing cries,
Heigh ho!

II.

Love is a torment of the mind,
A tempest everlasting:
And Jove hath made it of a kind,
Not well, nor full nor fasting.
Why so?
More we enjoy it, more it dies;
If not enjoyed, it sighing cries,
Heigh ho!

SAMUEL DANIEL.

SONG.

[1617?]

HAD Sorrow ever fitter place
To act his part,
Than is my heart,
Where it takes up all the space?
Where is no vein
To entertain
A thought that wears another face?

Nor will I Sorrow ever have
Therein to be,
But only thee,
To whom I full possession gave:
Thou in thy name
Must hold the same,
Until thou bring it to the grave.

SAMUEL DANIEL.

SONG.

[1618.]

I.

Rise, lady, miſtress, rise!
The night hath tedious been;
No ſleep hath fallen into my eyes,
Nor ſlumbers made me ſin:
Is not ſhe a saint then, say,
Thought of whom keeps ſin away?

II.

Rise, madam, rise, and give me light,
Whom darkness ſtill will cover,
And ignorance, darker than the night,
Till thou smile on thy lover:
All want day till thy beauty rise,
For the gray morn breaks from thine eyes.

NATHANIEL FIELD.

THE CRIER.

[1619.]

Good folk, for gold or hire,
But help me to a crier,
For my poor heart is run away,
After two eyes that paſſed this way.
O yes, O yes, O yes,

If there be any man,
In town or country, can
Bring me my heart again,
I'll please him for his pain;
And by these marks I will you show
That only I this heart do owe.
It is a wounded heart,
Wherein yet sticks the dart;
Every piece sore hurt throughout it,
Faith and troth writ round about it.
It was a tame heart, and a dear,
And never used to roam;
But having got this haunt, I fear
'Twill hardly stay at home.
For GOD'S *sake, walking by the way,*
If you my heart do see,
Either impound it for a stray,
Or send it back to me.

MICHAEL DRAYTON.

SONG.

[1620?]

I.

LADIES, flee from Love's sweet tale;
Oaths steeped in tears do oft prevail:
Grief is infectious, and the air,
Inflamed with sighs, will blast the fair.
Then stop your ears when lovers cry,
Lest yourself weeping with soft eye

Shall with a sorrowing tear repay
That pity which you cast away.

II.

Young men, flee when Beauty darts
Amorous glances at your hearts:
A quick eye gives the surer aim,
And ladies' lips have power to maim.
Now in her lips, now in her eyes,
Lapt in a kiss or smile, Love lies;
Then flee betimes, for only they
Do conquer Love that run away.

WILLIAM HERBERT, *Earl of Pembroke.*

SONG.

[1622.]

STAY, bold thoughts, refrain your will,
Silent be, and suffer still.
What! not speak, if she be by?
Torment; if you do, you die:
Say the flame to rise begin,
Tears without may quench within.
Better die in easy pain,
Suffering, than if not be slain.
Is there then no remedy?
Silence, then I'll welcome thee!
And thou, tongue of mine, conceal
What the heart must not reveal.

LEONARD DIGGES.

SONG.

[1622.]

I.

Come buy, you lusty gallants,
These simples which I sell:
In all our days were never seen like these,
For beauty, strength, and smell.
Here's the king-cup, the pansy, with the violet,
The rose that loves the shower,
The wholesome gilliflower,
Both the cowslip, lily,
And the daffadilly,
With a thousand in my power.

II.

Here's golden amaranthus,
That true love can provoke,
Of horehound store, and poisoning hellebore,
With the polipode of the oak:
Here's chaste vervine, and lustful eringo,
Health-preserving sage,
And rue, which cures old age,
With a world of others,
Making fruitful mothers;
All these attend me as my page.

Markham and Sampson.

SONG.

[1626?]

Drop golden showers, gentle Sleep,
And all the angels of the night,
Which do us in protection keep,
Make this queen dream of delight.
Morpheus, be kind a little, and be
Death's now true image, for 'twill prove
To this poor queen that thou art he;
Her grave is made i' the bed of love.
Thus with sweet sweets can Heaven mix gall,
And marriage turn to funeral.

THOMAS GOFFE.

SONG.

[1628.]

How I laugh at their fond wish,
Whose desire
Aims no higher
Than the baits of Midas' dish!

What is gold but yellow dirt,
Which th' unkind
Heavens refined,
When they made us love our hurt?

Would to Heaven that I might steep
My faint eyes
In the wise,
In the gentle dew of Sleep!

Whose effects do pose us so,
That we deem
It does seem
Both Death's brother and his foe.

This does always with us keep,
And being dead
That's not fled;
Death is but a longer Sleep.

ROBERT GOMERSALL.

A SONG,

FOR THE MUSIC LECTURE.

[1633.]

STRIKE again! O, no, no more,
I implore;
Such another touch would be
My destiny!
What bewitching sounds are these,
Which so please,
As that we begin to fear
What we hear?
Sound yet louder! Raise a tone,
Which to own
The celestial quire would be
Suitors t' ye.
Sound yet louder! that if Fate
Make this date

To my years, I yet may die
Speedily;
And that this ditty, sweetly ſtrong,
May be my death and funeral song.

ROBERT GOMERSALL.

SONG.

[1630.]

I.

WE care not for money, riches, or wealth,
Old Sack is our money, old Sack is our health:
Then let's flock hither,
Like birds of a feather,
To drink, to fling,
To laugh, to ſing,
Conferring our notes together,
Conferring our notes together.

II.

Come, let us laugh, let us drink, let us ſing,
The Winter with us is as good as the Spring:
We care not a feather
For wind, or for weather,
But night and day
We sport and play,
Conferring our notes together,
Conferring our notes together.

THOMAS RANDOLPH.

SONG.

[1631.]

Why art thou ſlow, thou reſt of trouble, Death,
To ſtop a wretch's breath,
That calls on thee, and offers her sad heart
A prey unto thy dart?
I am not young, nor fair; be, therefore, bold:
Sorrow hath made me old,
Deformed, and wrinkled; all that I can crave
Is quiet in my grave.
Such as live happy, hold long life a jewel;
But to me thou art cruel,
If thou end not my tedious misery,
And I soon cease to be.
Strike, and ſtrike home, then; pity unto me,
In one ſhort hour's delay, is tyranny.

Philip Massinger.

VIRTUE.

[1631?]

Sweet day, so cool, so calm, so bright,
The bridal of the earth and ſky;
The dew ſhall weep thy fall to-night,
For thou muſt die.

Sweet rose, whose hue, angry and brave,
Bids the raſh gazer wipe his eye;
Thy root is ever in its grave,
And thou muſt die.

Sweet Spring, full of sweet days and roses,
A box where sweets compacted lie;
My music shows ye have your closes,
And all must die.

Only a sweet and virtuous soul,
Like seasoned timber, never gives:
But though the whole world turns to coal,
Then chiefly lives.

GEORGE HERBERT.

DISDAIN RETURNED.

[1632.]

I.

He that loves a rosy cheek,
Or a coral lip admires,
Or, from star-like eyes, doth seek
Fuel to maintain his fires;
As old Time makes these decay,
So his flames must waste away.

II.

But a smooth and steadfast mind,
Gentle thoughts and calm desires,
Hearts, with equal love combined,
Kindle never-dying fires.
Where these are not, I despise
Lovely cheeks, or lips, or eyes.

THOMAS CAREW.

SONG.

[1636?]

I.

Ask me no more where Jove beſtows,
When June is paſt, the fading rose;
For in your beauty's orient deep,
These flowers, as in their causes, ſleep.

II.

Aſk me no more whither doth ſtray
The golden atoms of the day;
For, in pure love, Heaven did prepare
Those powders to enrich your hair.

III.

Aſk me no more whither doth haſte
The nightingale when Spring is paſt;
For in your sweet dividing throat
She winters, and keeps warm her note.

IV.

Aſk me no more where those ſtars light
That downwards fall in dead of night;
For in your eyes they ſit, and there
Fixed become as in their sphere.

V.

Aſk me no more if eaſt or weſt
The Phœnix builds her spicy neſt;
For unto you at laſt ſhe flies,
And in your fragrant bosom dies.

Thomas Carew.

SONG.

CELIA SINGING.

[1636?]

YOU that think love can convey
No other way,
But through the eyes, into the heart,
His fatal dart;
Close up those casements, and but hear
This siren sing;
And on the wing
Of her sweet voice it shall appear
That love can enter at the ear:
Then unveil your eyes, behold
The curious mould
Where that voice dwells; and, as we know,
When the cocks crow,
We freely may
Gaze on the day:
So may you, when the music's done,
Awake and see the rising sun.

THOMAS CAREW.

SONG.

[1633.]

OH, no more, no more, too late
Sighs are spent; the burning tapers
Of a life as chaste as fate,
Pure as are unwritten papers,

Are burned out: no heat, no light
Now remains; 'tis ever night.
Love is dead; let lovers' eyes,
Locked in endless dreams,
The extreme of all extremes,
Ope no more, for now love dies.
Now love dies, implying
Love's martyrs must be ever, ever dying.

JOHN FORD.

DIRGE.

[1633.]

GLORIES, *pleasures, pomps, delight, and ease,*
Can but please
The outward senses, when the mind
Is or untroubled, or by peace refined.
Crowns may flourish and decay,
Beauties shine, but fade away.
Youth may revel, yet it must
Lie down in a bed of dust.
Earthly honours flow and waste,
Time alone doth change and last.
Sorrows mingled with contents, prepare
Rest for care;
Love only reigns in death; though art
Can find no comfort for a broken heart.

JOHN FORD.

SONG.

[1634.]

O Sorrow, Sorrow, say where dost thou dwell?
In the lowest room of hell.
Art thou born of human race?
No, no, I have a fierier face!
Art thou in city, town, or court?
I to every place resort.
O, why into the world is Sorrow sent?
Men afflicted best repent.
What dost thou feed on?
Broken sleep.
What takest thou pleasure in?
To weep;
To sigh, to sob, to pine, to groan,
To wring my hands, to sit alone.
O when, O when shall Sorrow quiet have?
Never, never, never, never,
Never till she finds a grave.

Samuel Rowley.

TO ROSES IN THE BOSOM OF CASTARA.

[1634.]

I.

Ye, blushing virgins, happy are
In the chaste nunnery of her breasts;
For he'd profane so chaste a fair,
Whoe'er should call them Cupid's nests.

II.

Transplanted thus how bright ye grow,
How rich a perfume do ye yield!
In some close garden, cowslips so
Are sweeter than i' the open field.

III.

In those white cloisters live secure
From the rude blasts of wanton breath;
Each hour more innocent and pure,
Till you shall wither into death.

IV.

Then that which living gave you room,
Your glorious sepulchre shall be:
There wants no marble for a tomb,
Whose heart hath marble been to me.

WILLIAM HABINGTON.

UPON CASTARA'S DEPARTURE.

[1634.]

VOWS are vain. No suppliant breath
Stays the speed of swift-heeled Death.
Life with her is gone, and I
Learn but a new way to die.
See, the flowers condole, and all
Wither in my funeral.
The bright lily, as if day
Parted with her, fades away.

Violets hang their heads, and lose
All their beauty That the rose
A sad part in sorrow bears,
Witness all those dewy tears,
Which as pearl, or diamond-like,
Swell upon her blushing cheek.
All things mourn. But O, behold
How the withered marigold
Closeth up now she is gone,
Judging her the setting Sun!

WILLIAM HABINGTON.

SONG.

[1634.]

SWEET Echo, sweetest nymph, that liv'st unseen
Within thy airy shell,
By slow Meander's margent green,
And in the violet-embroidered vale,
Where the love-lorn nightingale
Nightly to thee her sad song mourneth well;
Canst thou not tell me of a gentle pair
That likest thy Narcissus are?
O, if thou have
Hid them in some flowery cave,
Tell me but where,
Sweet queen of parley, daughter of the sphere!
So mayst thou be translated to the skies,
And give resounding grace to all heaven's harmonies.

JOHN MILTON.

SONG.

[1634.]

SABRINA fair,
Liſten where thou art ſitting
Under the glaſſy, cool, tranſlucent wave,
In twiſted braids of lilies knitting
The loose train of thy amber-dropping hair;
Liſten for dear honour's sake,
Goddess of the ſilver lake,
Liſten and save.
Liſten and appear to us
In name of great Oceanus,
By th' earth-ſhaking Neptune's mace,
And Tethys' grave majeſtic face,
By hoary Nereus' wrinkled look,
And the Carpathian wizard's hook,
By scaly Triton's winding ſhell,
And old soothsaying Glaucus' spell,
By Leucothea's lovely hands,
And her son that rules the ſtrands,
By Thetis' tinsel-ſlippered feet,
And the songs of Sirens sweet,
By dead Parthenope's dear tomb,
And fair Ligea's golden comb,
Wherewith ſhe ſits on diamond rocks,
Sleeking her soft alluring locks,
By all the nymphs that nightly dance
Upon thy ſtreams with wily glance,
Rise, rise, and heave thy rosy head
From thy coral-paven bed,

And bridle in thy headlong wave,
Till thou our summons answered have.
Liſten and save.

John Milton.

SONG.

[1638.]

I.

While Morpheus thus does gently lay
His powerful charge upon each part,
Making thy spirits even obey
The ſilver charms of his dull art;

II.

I, thy Good Angel, from thy ſide,
As smoke doth from the altar rise,
Making no noise as it doth glide,
Will leave thee in this soft surprise;

III.

And from the clouds will fetch thee down
A holy viſion, to express
Thy right unto an earthly crown;
No power can make this kingdom less.

IV.

But gently, gently, leſt I bring
A ſtart in ſleep by sudden flight,
Playing aloof, and hovering,
Till I am loſt unto the ſight.

V.

This is a motion ſtill and soft:
So free from noise and cry,
That Jove himself, who hears a thought,
Knows not when we pass by.

HENRY KILLIGREW.

SONG.

[1638.]

I.

WHY so pale and wan, fond lover?
Prithee why so pale?
Will, when looking well can't move her,
Looking ill prevail?
Prithee why so pale?

II.

Why so dull and mute, young ſinner?
Prithee why so mute?
Will, when speaking well can't win her,
Saying nothing do't?
Prithee why so mute?

III.

Quit, quit for ſhame, this will not move,
This cannot take her;
If of herself ſhe will not love,
Nothing can make her:
The devil take her!

SIR JOHN SUCKLING.

SONG.

[1640?]

I.

OUT upon it, I have loved
Three whole days together;
And am like to love three more,
If it prove fair weather!

II.

Time ſhall moult away his wings,
Ere he ſhall discover,
In the whole wide world again,
Such a conſtant lover.

III.

But the spite on't is, no praise
Is due at all to me:
Love with me had made no ſtays,
Had it any been but ſhe.

IV.

Had it any been but ſhe,
And that very face,
There had been at leaſt ere this
A dozen dozen in her place!

SIR JOHN SUCKLING.

OF A MISTRESS

OF WHOSE AFFECTION HE WAS DOUBTFUL.

[1639.]

What though with figures I ſhould raise
Above all height my miſtress' praise;
Calling her cheek a bluſhing rose,
The faireſt June did e'er disclose;
Her forehead, lilies; and her eyes,
The luminaries of the ſkies:
That on her lips ambroſia grows,
And from her kiſſes nectar flows?
Too great hyperboles, unless
She loves me, ſhe is none of these.
But if her heart and her deſires
Do answer mine with equal fires,
These attributes are then too poor:
She is all these, and ten times more.

Thomas Nabbes.

SONG.

[1639.]

I.

Unclose those eyelids, and outſhine
The brightness of the breaking day!
The light they cover is divine;
Why ſhould it fade so soon away?
Stars vaniſh so, and day appears;
The sun's so drowned i' the morning's tears.

II.

O, let not sadness cloud this beauty,
Which if you lose you'll ne'er recover!
It is not Love's, but Sorrow's duty,
To die so soon for a dead lover.
Banish, O, banish grief, and then
Our joys will bring our hopes again.

HENRY GLAPTHORNE.

OUT OF THE ITALIAN.

[1640?]

I.

To thy lover,
Dear, discover
That sweet blush of thine that shameth
(When those roses
It discloses)
All the flowers that Nature nameth.

II.

In free air
Flow thy hair,
That no more Summer's best dresses
Be beholden
For their golden
Locks to Phœbus' flaming tresses.

III.

O deliver
Love his quiver;
From thy eyes he shoots his arrows,

Where Apollo
Cannot follow,
Feathered with his mother's sparrows.

IV.

O envy not
(That we die not)
Those dear lips whose door encloses
All the Graces
In their places,
Brother pearls, and fister roses!

V.

From these treasures
Of ripe pleasures
One bright smile to clear the weather:
Earth and heaven,
Thus made even,
Both will be good friends together.

VI.

The air does woo thee,
Winds cling to thee;
Might a word once fly from out thee,
Storm and thunder
Would fit under,
And keep filence round about thee.

VII.

But if Nature's
Common creatures
So dear glories dare not borrow;

Yet thy beauty
Owes a duty
To my loving, lingering sorrow.

VIII.

When to end me
Death ſhall send me
All his terrors to affright me:
Thine eyes' graces
Gild their faces,
And those terrors ſhall delight me.

IX.

When my dying
Life is flying,
Those sweet airs that often ſlew me
Shall revive me,
Or reprieve me,
And to many deaths renew me.

RICHARD CRASHAW.

DIRGE.

[1640.]

NOBLEST bodies are but gilded clay.
Put away
But the precious ſhining rind,
The inmoſt rottenness remains behind.
Kings, on earth though gods they be,
Yet in death are vile as we.

He, a thousand kings before,
Now is vassal unto more.
Vermin now insulting lie,
And dig for diamonds in each eye;
Whilst the sceptre-bearing hand
Cannot their inroads withstand.
Here doth one in odours wade,
By the regal unction made;
While another dares to gnaw
On that tongue, his people's law.
Fools, ah! fools are we that so contrive,
And do strive,
In each gaudy ornament,
Who shall his corpse in the best dish present.

SICILY AND NAPLES: A TRAGEDY.

TO CYNTHIA,
ON CONCEALMENT OF HER BEAUTY.

[1641.]

I.

Do not conceal thy radiant eyes,
The star-light of serenest skies;
Lest, wanting of their heavenly light,
They turn to Chaos' endless night!

II.

Do not conceal those tresses fair,
The silken snares of thy curled hair;
Lest, finding neither gold nor ore,
The curious silk-worm work no more!

III.

Do not conceal those breaſts of thine,
More snow-white than the Apennine;
Leſt, if there be like snow and froſt,
The lily be forever loſt!

IV.

Do not conceal that fragrant scent,
Thy breath, which to all flowers hath lent
Perfumes; leſt, it being suppreſt,
No spices grow in all the Eaſt!

V.

Do not conceal thy heavenly voice,
Which makes the hearts of gods rejoice;
Leſt, muſic hearing no such thing,
The nightingale forget to ſing!

VI.

Do not conceal, nor yet eclipse
Thy pearly teeth with coral lips;
Leſt that the seas cease to bring forth
Gems which from thee have all their worth!

VII.

Do not conceal no beauty, grace,
That's either in thy mind or face;
Leſt virtue overcome by vice
Make men believe no Paradise!

Sir Francis Kinaston.

SONG.

[1642.]

Morpheus, the humble God, that dwells
In cottages and smoky cells,
Hates gilded roofs, and beds of down;
And though he fears no prince's frown,
Flies from the circle of a crown.

Come, I say, thou powerful God,
And thy leaden charming rod,
Dipped in the Lethean lake,
O'er his wakeful temples ſhake,
Leſt he ſhould ſleep, and never wake.

Nature, alas! why art thou so
Obliged to thy greateſt foe?
Sleep, that is thy beſt repaſt,
Yet of death it bears a taſte,
And both are the same thing at laſt.

Sir John Denham.

TO ALTHEA.

FROM PRISON.

[1642.]

When Love with unconfined wings
Hovers within my gates;
And my divine Althea brings
To whisper at the grates:

When I lie tangled in her hair,
And fettered to her eye,
The birds, that wanton in the air,
Know no such liberty.

When flowing cups run swiftly round
With no allaying Thames,
Our careless heads with roses bound,
Our hearts with loyal flames;
When thirſty grief in wine we ſteep,
When healths and draughts go free,
Fiſhes, that tipple in the deep,
Know no such liberty.

When, like committed linnets, I
With ſhriller throat ſhall ſing
The sweetness, mercy, majeſty,
And glories of my King;
When I ſhall voice aloud how good
He is, how great ſhould be,
Enlarged winds, that curl the flood,
Know no such liberty.

Stone walls do not a prison make,
Nor iron bars a cage;
Minds innocent and quiet take
That for an hermitage:
If I have freedom in my love,
And in my soul am free,
Angels alone, that soar above,
Enjoy such liberty.

RICHARD LOVELACE.

SONG.

TO LUCASTA. GOING TO THE WARS.

[1646.]

TELL me not, sweet, I am unkind,
That from the nunnery
Of thy chaſte breaſt and quiet mind
To war and arms I fly.

True, a new miſtress now I chase,
The firſt foe in the field;
And with a ſtronger faith embrace
A sword, a horse, a ſhield.

Yet this inconſtancy is such
As you too ſhall adore:
I could not love thee, dear, so much,
Loved I not Honour more.

RICHARD LOVELACE.

A VALEDICTION.

[1642?]

BID me not go where neither sun nor ſhowers
Do make or cheriſh flowers;
Where discontented things in sadness lie,
And Nature grieves as I.
When I am parted from those eyes,
From which my better day doth rise,
Though some propitious Power
Should plant me in a bower,

Where amongst happy lovers I might see
How showers and sunbeams bring
One everlasting Spring,
Nor would those fall, nor these shine forth to me:
Nature herself to him is lost,
Who loseth her he honours most.
Then, fairest, to my parting view display
Your graces all in one full day:
Whose blessed shapes I'll snatch and keep, till when
I do return and view agen:
So by this art Fancy shall Fortune cross,
And lovers live by thinking on their loss.

WILLIAM CARTWRIGHT.

ON A GIRDLE.

[1645.]

THAT which her slender waist confined,
Shall now my joyful temples bind;
No monarch but would give his crown,
His arms might do what this has done.

It was my heaven's extremest sphere,
The pale which held that lovely deer.
My joy, my grief, my hope, my love,
Did all within this circle move!

A narrow compass, and yet there
Dwelt all that's good, and all that's fair.
Give me but what this ribbon bound,
Take all the rest the sun goes round.

EDMUND WALLER.

GO, LOVELY ROSE.

[1645.]

I.

Go, lovely Rose!
Tell her that wastes her time and me,
That now she knows,
When I resemble her to thee,
How sweet and fair she seems to be.

II.

Tell her that's young,
And shuns to have her graces spied,
That hadst thou sprung
In deserts, where no men abide,
Thou must have uncommended died.

III.

Small is the worth
Of beauty from the light retired;
Bid her come forth,
Suffer herself to be desired,
And not blush so to be admired.

IV.

Then die, that she
The common fate of all things rare
May read in thee;
How small a part of Time they share
That are so wondrous sweet and fair!

EDMUND WALLER.

THE PASSING-BELL.

[1646.]

HARK! how chimes the paſſing-bell,
There's no muſic to a knell:
All the other sounds we hear
Flatter, and but cheat our ear.
This doth put us ſtill in mind
That our fleſh muſt be reſigned,
And a general ſilence made,
The world be muffled in a ſhade.
He that on his pillow lies,
Tear-embalmed before he dies,
Carries, like a ſheep, his life
To meet the sacrificer's knife,
And for Eternity is preſt,
Sad bell-wether to the reſt.

JAMES SHIRLEY.

SONG.

[1659.]

I.

THE glories of our blood and ſtate
Are ſhadows, not subſtantial things;
There is no armour againſt Fate;
Death lays his icy hand on kings:
Sceptre and crown
Muſt tumble down,
And in the duſt be equal made
With the poor crooked scythe and spade.

II.

Some men with swords may reap the field,
And plant fresh laurels where they kill;
But their strong nerves at last must yield;
They tame but one another still:
Early or late
They stoop to Fate,
And must give up their murmuring breath,
When they, pale captives, creep to death.

III.

The garlands wither on your brow,
Then boast no more your mighty deeds;
Upon Death's purple altar now
See, where the victor victim bleeds:
Your heads must come
To the cold tomb;
Only the actions of the just
Smell sweet, and blossom in their dust.

James Shirley.

SONG.

CELIA IN LOVE.

[1646.]

I FELT my heart, and found a flame,
That for relief and shelter came:
I entertained the treacherous guest,
And gave it welcome in my breast.

Poor Celia! whither wilt thou go?
To cool in ſtreams, or freeze in snow?
Or gentle Zephyrus entreat,
To chill thy flames, and fan thy heat?
Perhaps a taper's fading beams
May die in air, or quench in ſtreams;
But love is a myſterious fire,
Nor can in air or ice expire:
Nor will this Phœnix be ſuppreſt
But with the ruin of his neſt.

MARTIN LLUELLIN.

HONOUR.

[1647.]

I.

SHE *loves, and she confeſſes too;*
There's then at laſt no more to do.
The happy work's entirely done,
Enter the town which thou haſt won;
The fruits of conqueſt now begin:
Io Triumphe! Enter in.

II.

What's this, ye gods! what can it be?
Remains there ſtill an enemy?
Bold Honour ſtands up in the gate,
And would yet capitulate.
Have I o'ercome all real foes,
And ſhall this Phantom me oppose?

III.

Noisy Nothing! ſtalking Shade!
By what witchcraft wert thou made?
Empty cause of solid harms!
But I ſhall find out counter-charms
Thy airy Devilſhip to remove
From this circle here of Love.

IV.

Sure I ſhall rid myself of thee,
By the Night's obscurity,
And obscurer Secrecy.
Unlike to every other sprite,
Thou attempt'ſt not men t' affright,
Nor appear'ſt but in the Light.

ABRAHAM COWLEY.

CHERRY-RIPE.

[1648.]

CHERRY-RIPE, ripe, ripe, I cry,
Full and fair ones, come and buy
If so be you aſk me where
They do grow, I answer, There,
Where my Julia's lips do smile;
There's the land, or cherry-iſle,
Whose plantations fully ſhow
All the year where cherries grow.

ROBERT HERRICK.

TO MEADOWS.

[1648.]

I.

YE have been fresh and green,
Ye have been filled with flowers;
And ye the walks have been
Where maids have spent their hours.

II.

Ye have beheld how they
With wicker arks did come,
To kiss and bear away
The richer cowslips home.

III.

Y'ave heard them sweetly sing,
And seen them in a round:
Each virgin, like a Spring,
With honeysuckles crowned.

IV.

But now we see none here
Whose silvery feet did tread,
And with dishevelled hair
Adorned this smoother mead.

V.

Like unthrifts, having spent
Your stock, and needy grown,
Y'are left here to lament
Your poor estates, alone.

ROBERT HERRICK.

TO PRIMROSES FILLED WITH MORNING DEW.

[1648.]

Why do ye weep, sweet babes? Can tears
Speak grief in you,
Who were but born
Just as the modest Morn
Teemed her refreshing dew?
Alas! ye have not known that shower
That mars a flower;
Nor felt th' unkind
Breath of a blasting wind;
Nor are ye worn with years,
Or warped, as we,
Who think it strange to see
Such pretty flowers, like to orphans young,
To speak by tears before ye have a tongue.

Speak, whimpering younglings, and make known
The reason why
Ye droop and die.
Is it for want of sleep,
Or childish lullaby?
Or that ye have not seen as yet
The violet?
Or brought a kiss
From that sweet heart to this?
No, no, this sorrow shown
By your tears shed,
Would have this lecture read:
That things of greatest, so of meanest worth,
Conceived with grief are, and with tears brought forth.

Robert Herrick.

TO DAFFODILS.

[1648.]

I.

Fair daffodils, we weep to see
You haste away so soon:
As yet the early-rising sun
Has not attained his noon.
Stay, stay,
Until the hasting day
Has run
But to the even-song;
And, having prayed together, we
Will go with you along.

II.

We have short time to stay as you,
We have as short a Spring;
As quick a growth to meet decay,
As you, or any thing.
We die,
As your hours do, and dry
Away
Like to the Summer's rain;
Or as the pearls of morning dew,
Ne'er to be found again.

Robert Herrick.

TO BLOSSOMS.

[1648.]

I.

FAIR pledges of a fruitful tree,
Why do ye fall so fast?
Your date is not so past,
But you may stay yet here awhile,
To blush and gently smile,
And go at last.

II.

What, were ye born to be
An hour or half's delight,
And so to bid good-night?
'Twas pity Nature brought ye forth
Merely to show your worth,
And lose you quite.

III.

But you are lovely leaves, where we
May read how soon things have
Their end, though ne'er so brave;
And after they have shown their pride,
Like you, awhile, they glide
Into the grave.

ROBERT HERRICK.

TO VIRGINS,

TO MAKE MUCH OF TIME.

[1648.]

I.

GATHER ye rose-buds while ye may,
Old Time is ſtill a-flying,
And this same flower that smiles to-day,
To-morrow will be dying.

II.

The glorious lamp of Heaven, the Sun,
The higher he's a-getting,
The sooner will his race be run,
And nearer he's to setting.

III.

That age is beſt which is the firſt,
When youth and blood are warmer;
But being spent, the worse, and worſt
Times ſtill succeed the former.

IV.

Then be not coy, but use your time,
And while ye may, go marry;
For having loſt but once your prime,
You may forever tarry.

ROBERT HERRICK.

THE NIGHT-PIECE, TO JULIA.

[1648.]

I.

HER eyes the glow-worm lend thee,
The shooting stars attend thee;
And the elves also,
Whose little eyes glow
Like the sparks of fire, befriend thee.

II.

No Will-o'-th'-Wisp mis-light thee,
Nor snake or slow-worm bite thee;
But on, on thy way,
Not making a stay,
Since ghost there's none to affright thee.

III.

Let not the dark thee cumber;
What though the moon does slumber?
The stars of the night
Will lend thee their light,
Like tapers clear without number.

IV.

Then, Julia, let me woo thee,
Thus, thus to come unto me:
And when I shall meet
Thy silvery feet,
My soul I'll pour into thee.

ROBERT HERRICK.

TO THE WESTERN WIND.

[1648.]

SWEET weſtern wind, whose luck it is,
Made rival with the air,
To give Perenna's lip a kiss,
And fan her wanton hair,

Bring me but one, I'll promise thee,
Inſtead of common ſhowers,
Thy wings ſhall be embalmed by me,
And all beset with flowers.

ROBERT HERRICK.

TO THE WATER-NYMPHS
DRINKING AT THE FOUNTAIN.

[1648.]

I.

REACH with your whiter hands to me
Some cryſtal of the spring,
And I about the cup ſhall see
Freſh lilies flouriſhing.

II.

Or else, sweet nymphs, do you but this—
To th' glass your lips incline,
And I ſhall see, by that one kiss,
The water turned to wine!

ROBERT HERRICK.

TO ELECTRA.

[1648.]

I.

I DARE not ask a kiss,
I dare not beg a smile;
Lest, having that or this,
I might grow proud the while.

II.

No, no, the utmost share
Of my desire shall be,
Only to kiss the air
That lately kissed thee.

ROBERT HERRICK.

SONG.

[1649?]

I.

DEAR, do not your fair beauty wrong,
In thinking still you are too young;
The rose and lilies in your cheek
Flourish, and no more ripeness seek.

II.

Your cherry lip, red, soft, and sweet,
Proclaims such fruit for taste most meet;
Then lose no time, for Love has wings,
And flies away from aged things.

THOMAS MAY.

THE RETREAT.

[1650.]

HAPPY those early days, when I
Shined in my angel-infancy!
Before I underſtood this place
Appointed for my second race,
Or taught my soul to fancy aught
But a white, celeſtial thought:
When yet I had not walked above
A mile or two from my firſt love,
And looking back, at that ſhort space,
Could see a glimpse of his bright face;
When on some gilded cloud, or flower,
My gazing soul would dwell an hour,
And in those weaker glories spy
Some ſhadows of eternity;
Before I taught my tongue to wound
My conscience with a ſinful sound,
Or had the black art to dispense
A several ſin to every sense,
But felt through all this fleſhly dress
Bright ſhoots of everlaſtingness.
   O how I long to travel back
And tread again that ancient track!
That I might once more reach that plain,
Where firſt I left my glorious train;
From whence th' enlightened spirit sees
That ſhady city of palm-trees.
But ah, my soul with too much ſtay
Is drunk, and ſtaggers in the way!

Some men a forward motion love,
But I by backward ſteps would move,
And when this duſt falls to the urn,
In that ſtate I came return.

HENRY VAUGHAN.

THE SHOWER.

[1650?]

WATERS above, eternal springs,
The dew that ſilvers the Dove's wings!
O welcome, welcome to the sad!
Give dry duſt drink, drink that makes glad.
Many fair evenings, many flowers
Sweetened with rich and gentle ſhowers,
Have I enjoyed; and down have run
Many a fine and ſhining sun:
But never, till this happy hour,
Was bleſt with such an evening ſhower!

HENRY VAUGHAN.

SONG.

[1650?]

COME, ye young men, come along,
With your muſic, dance, and song;
Bring your laſſes in your hands,
For 'tis that which Love commands.

Then to the Maypole come away,
For it is now a holiday.

It is the choice time of the year,
For the violets now appear;
Now the rose receives its birth,
And pretty primrose decks the earth.
Then to the Maypole come away,
For it is now a holiday.

Here each bachelor may choose
One that will not faith abuse,
Nor repay with cold disdain,
Love that ſhould be loved again.
Then to the Maypole come away,
For it is now a holiday.

And when you well reckoned have,
What kiſſes you your sweethearts gave,
Take them all again, and more,
It will never make them poor.
Then to the Maypole come away,
For it is now a holiday.

When you thus have spent the time,
Till the day be paſt its prime,
To your beds repair at night,
And dream there of your day's delight.
Then to the Maypole come away,
For it is now a holiday.

Robert Cox.

THE EXEQUIES.

[1651.]

Draw near,
You lovers that complain
Of Fortune or Disdain,
And to my aſhes lend a tear;
Melt the hard marble with your groans,
And soften the relentless ſtones,
Whose cold embraces the sad subject hide,
Of all Love's cruelties, and Beauty's pride.

No verse,
No epicedium bring,
Nor peaceful requiem ſing,
To charm the terrors of my hearse;
No profane numbers muſt flow near
The sacred ſilence that dwells here.
Vaſt griefs are dumb; softly, O, softly mourn,
Leſt you diſturb the peace attends my urn.

Yet ſtrew
Upon my dismal grave
Such offerings as you have,
Forsaken cypress and sad yew;
For kinder flowers can take no birth,
Or growth, from such unhappy earth.
Weep only o'er my duſt, and say, Here lies
To Love and Fate an equal sacrifice.

Thomas Stanley.

LOVE ONCE, LOVE EVER.

[1651.]

SHALL I, hopeless, then pursue
A fair ſhadow that ſtill flies me?
Shall I ſtill adore, and woo
A proud heart that does despise me?
I a conſtant love may so,
But, alas! a fruitless ſhow.

Shall I by the erring light
Of two croſſer ſtars ſtill sail?
That do ſhine, but ſhine in spite,
Not to guide, but make me fail?
I a wandering course may ſteer,
But the harbour ne'er come near.

Whilſt these thoughts my soul poſſess,
Reason paſſion would o'ersway,
Bidding me my flames suppress,
Or divert some other way:
But what reason would pursue,
That my heart runs counter to.

So a pilot, bent to make
Search for some unfound-out land,
Does with him the magnet take,
Sailing to the unknown ſtrand:
But that, ſteer which way he will,
To the loved North points ſtill.

SIR EDWARD SHERBURNE.

SONG.

[1652?]

He's great that masters his own soul,
As he whose nod shakes either Pole.
Not he that kings in chains can bring,
But that subdues himself's a king;
That's ever in himself at home,
And ne'er lets his queen, Reason, roam,
On whom all passions waiting stand,
As handmaids on their lady's hand.
He o'er himself triumphing first,
Dares Chance and Envy do their worst;
And keeping still his own even height,
Fall Fortune heavy, fall she light,
He'll never make to th' standers by
Too low a moan, or haughty cry;
But wisely can her fawning slight,
And then as bravely scorn her spite.
Who can deny that such a one
Possesses all things, or wants none?
And which o' th' two would you wish first,
Still to have drink, or ne'er to thirst?

Robert Baron.

THE ANGLER'S WISH.

[1653.]

I.

I in these flowery meads would be:
These crystal streams should solace me;

To whose harmonious bubbling noise
I with my angle would rejoice:
Sit here, and see the turtle-dove
Court his chaste mate to acts of love.

II.

Or, on that bank, feel the west wind
Breathe health and plenty; please my mind
To see sweet dew-drops kiss these flowers,
And then, washed off by April showers:
Here, hear my Kenna sing a song;
There, see a blackbird feed her young;

III.

Or a leverock build her nest;
Here, give my weary spirits rest,
And raise my low-pitched thoughts above
Earth, or what poor mortals love:
Thus free from law-suits, and the noise
Of princes' courts, I would rejoice.

IV.

Or, with my Bryan, and a book,
Loiter long days near Shawford brook:
There sit by him, and eat my meat,
There see the sun both rise and set:
There bid good-morning to next day,
There meditate my time away:
And angle on, and beg to have
A quiet passage to a welcome grave.

Izaak Walton.

AMINTOR'S WELL-A-DAY.

[1653.]

CHLORIS, now thou art fled away,
Amintor's sheep are gone astray,
And all the joy he took to see
His pretty lambs run after thee,
Is gone, is gone, and he alway
Sings nothing now but well-a-day!

His oaten pipe, that in thy praise
Was wont to sing such roundelays,
Is thrown away, and not a swain
Dares pipe, or sing, within his plain;
'Tis death for any now to say
One word to him but well-a-day!

The May-pole where thy little feet
So roundly did in measures meet,
Is broken down, and no content
Comes near Amintor since you went.
All that I ever heard him say,
Was Chloris, Chloris, well-a-day!

Upon these banks you used to tread,
He ever since hath lain his head,
And whispered there such pining woe,
As not a blade of grass will grow.
O Chloris, Chloris, come away,
And hear Amintor's well-a-day!

H. HUGHES.

TO AMANDA,

LEAVING HIM ALONE.

[1653.]

WHAT business calls thee hence, and calls not me?
My business ever is to wait on thee;
Therefore where'er you go,
I must go too;
Whate'er your business is,
Be it that, or this,
Yet still my business is to wait on you.
Nay, prithee, my dearest, why
So coy and shy?
Yes, yes, you'll come agen,
But, prithee, when?
Here must I mope alone,
Whilst you some other love,
Or, in your cabinet above,
Some letters doat upon,
Which teach you how to say me Nay.
But know, Amanda, if too long you stay,
My soul shall vanish into air,
And haunt and dodge thee everywhere.
'Tis fit when thou tak'st Heaven from me,
Thou take at least my soul with thee.

N. HOOKES.

SONG.

[1654.]

SOLITUDE, of friends the beſt,
And the beſt companion;
Mother of truths, and brought at leaſt
Every day to bed of one;
In this flowery manſion
I contemplate how the rose
Stands upon thorns, how quickly goes
The dismaying jeſſamine:
Only the soul, which is divine,
No decay of beauty knows.
The World is Beauty's Mirror. Flowers,
In their firſt virgin purity,
Flatterers both of the nose and eye—
To be cropped by paramours
Is their beſt of deſtiny:
And those nice darlings of the land,
Which seemed heaven's painted bow to scorn,
And bloomed the envy of the morn,
Are the gay trophy of a hand.

SIR RICHARD FANSHAW.

SONG.

[1654.]

STILL-BORN Silence, thou that art
Floodgate of the deeper heart;
Offspring of a heavenly kind;
Frost o' th' mouth, and thaw o' th' mind;
Secrecy's confident, and he
That makes religion Mystery:
Admiration's speaking'st tongue,—
Leave thy desert shades, among
Reverend hermits' hallowed cells,
Where retired'st Devotion dwells:
With thy enthusiasms come;
Seize this maid, and make her dumb.

RICHARD FLECKNOE.

ON CHLORIS WALKING IN THE SNOW.

[1654.]

I SAW fair Chloris walk alone,
When feathered rain came softly down;
Then Jove descended from his tower,
To woo her in a silver shower.
The wanton snow flew to her breast,
Like little birds into their nest;
But overcome with whiteness there,
For grief it thawed into a tear:
Then falling down her garment hem,
To deck her, froze into a gem.

WIT'S RECREATIONS.

SONG.

[1657.]

I.

Tell me no more how fair ſhe is,
I have no mind to hear
The ſtory of that diſtant bliss
I never ſhall come near:
By sad experience I have found
That her perfection is my wound.

II.

And tell me not how fond I am
To tempt a daring fate,
From whence no triumph ever came,
But to repent too late:
There is some hope ere long I may
In ſilence dote myself away.

III.

I aſk no pity, love, from thee,
Nor will thy juſtice blame,
So that thou wilt not envy me
The glory of my flame:
Which crowns my heart whene'er it dies,
In that it falls her sacrifice.

Henry King, *Biſhop of Chicheſter.*

FAIRY SONG.

[1658.]

COME, follow, follow me,
You, fairy elves that be,
Which circle on the green,
Come, follow Mab, your Queen.
Hand in hand let's dance around,
For this place is fairy ground.

When mortals are at reſt,
And snoring in their neſt,
Unheard, and unespied,
Through keyholes we do glide;
Over tables, ſtools, and ſhelves,
We trip it with our fairy elves.

And if the house be foul
With platter, diſh, or bowl,
Up ſtairs we nimbly creep,
And find the ſluts aſleep:
There we pinch their arms and thighs;
None escapes, nor none espies.

But if the house be swept,
And from uncleanness kept,
We praise the household maid,
And duly ſhe is paid;
For we use, before we go,
To drop a teſter in her ſhoe.

Upon a muſhroom's head
Our table-cloth we spread;
A grain of rye or wheat
Is manchet which we eat;
Pearly drops of dew we drink,
In acorn-cups filled to the brink.

The brains of nightingales,
With unctuous fat of snails,
Between two cockles ſtewed,
Is meat that's eaſily chewed;
Tails of worms, and marrow of mice,
Do make a diſh that's wondrous nice.

The grasshopper, gnat, and fly,
Serve us for our minſtrelsy;
Grace said, we dance awhile,
And so the time beguile;
And if the moon doth hide her head,
The glow-worm lights us home to bed.

On tops of dewy grass
So nimbly do we pass,
The young and tender ſtalk
Ne'er bends when we do walk:
Yet in the morning may be seen
Where we the night before have been.

MYSTERIES OF LOVE AND ELOQUENCE.

SONG.

[1660.]

Cupid all his arts did prove
To invite my heart to love;
But I always did delay
His mild summons to obey,
Being deaf to all his charms.
Straight the god aſſumes his arms:
With his bow and quiver, he
Takes the field to duel me.
Armed like Achilles, I
With my ſhield alone defy
His bold challenge; as he caſt
His golden darts, I as faſt
Catched his arrows in my ſhield,
Till I made him leave the field:
Fretting and disarmed then,
The angry god returns agen
All his flames; 'ſtead of a dart,
Throws himself into my heart:
Useless I my ſhield require,
When the fort is all on fire;
I in vain the field did win,
Now the enemy's within.
Thus betrayed, at laſt I cry,
Love, thou haſt the victory.

Thomas Ford.

TO THE INCONSTANT CYNTHIA.

[1660.]

I.

TELL me once, dear, how it does prove
That I so much forsworn could be?
I never swore always to love,
I only vowed ſtill to love thee.
And art thou now what thou wert then,
Unsworn unto by other men?

II.

In thy fair breaſt, and once-fair soul,
I thought my vows were writ alone;
But others' oaths so blurred the scroll,
That I no more could read my own.
And am I ſtill obliged to pay,
When you had thrown the bond away?

III.

Nor muſt we only part in joy,
Our tears as well muſt be unkind:
Weep you, that could such truth deſtroy,
And I that could such falseness find.
Thus we muſt unconcerned remain
In our divided joys and pain.

Yet we may love, but on this different score,
You, what I am, I, what you were before.

SIR ROBERT HOWARD.

SONG.

[1661.]

I.

COME, Somnus, with thy potent charms,
And seize this captive in thy arms;
And sweetly drop on every sense
Thy soul-refreshing influence.
His sight, smell, hearing, touch, and taste,
Unto thy peace do thou bind fast.

II.

On working brains, at school all day,
At night thou dost bestow a play;
And troubled minds thou dost set free;
Thou mak'st both friends and foes agree:
All are alike, who live by breath,
In thee, and in thy brother Death.

PHILONAX LOVEKIN.

SONG.

[1664.]

I.

LADIES, though to your conquering eyes
Love owes his chiefest victories,
And borrows those bright arms from you
With which he does the world subdue;
Yet you yourselves are not above
The empire nor the griefs of love.

II.

Then rack not lovers with disdain,
Lest Love on you revenge their pain;
You are not free because you're fair,
The boy did not his mother spare;
Though beauty be a killing dart,
It is no armour for the heart.

SIR GEORGE ETHEREGE.

THE RESOLVE.

[1664.]

I.

TELL me not of a face that's fair,
Nor lip nor cheek that's red;
Nor of the tresses of her hair,
Nor curls in order laid:
Nor of a rare seraphic voice,
That like an angel sings:
Though if I were to take my choice,
I would have all these things.
But if thou wilt have me love,
And it must be a she,
The only argument can move,
Is, that she will love me.

II.

The glories of your ladies be
But metaphors of things;
And but resemble what we see
Each common object brings.

Roses out-red their lips and cheeks,
Lilies their whiteness ſtain:
What fool is he that ſhadows seeks,
And may the subſtance gain?
Then if thou'lt have me love a lass,
Let it be one that's kind;
Else I'm a servant to the glass
That's with Canary lined.

ALEXANDER BROME.

ON CLARET.

[1664.]

WITHIN this bottle's to be seen
A scarlet liquor, that has been
Born of the royal Vine;
We but nick-name it when we call
It Gods' drink, who drink none at all—
No higher name than Wine.

'Tis ladies' liquor: here one might
Feaſt both his eye and appetite,
With beauty and with taſte;
Cherries and roses, which you seek
Upon your miſtress' lip and cheek,
Are here together placed.

Phyſicians may prescribe their whey,
To purge our reins and brains away,
And clarify the blood;

That cures one sickness with another,
This routs by wholesale altogether,
And drowns them in a flood.

This poets makes, else how could I
Thus ramble into poetry,
Nay, and write sonnets too?
If there's such power in junior wines,
To make one venture upon lines,
What could Canary do?

Then squeeze the vessel's bowels out,
And deal it faithfully about,—
Crown each hand with a brimmer:
Since we're to pass through this Red Sea,
Our noses shall our pilots be,
And every soul a swimmer!

ALEXANDER BROME.

SONG.

THE SOLDIER GOING TO THE FIELD.

[1666?]

PRESERVE thy sighs, unthrifty girl,
To purify the air:
Thy tears to thread instead of pearl
On bracelets of thy hair.

The trumpet makes the echo hoarse,
And wakes the louder drum;
Expense of grief gains no remorse,
When sorrow should be dumb.

For I muſt go where lazy Peace
Will hide her drowsy head,
And, for the sport of kings, increase
The number of the dead!

But firſt I'll chide thy cruel theſt.
Can I in war delight,
Who being of my heart bereſt
Can have no heart to fight?

Thou know'ſt the sacred laws of old
Ordained a thief ſhould pay,
To quit him of his theſt, seven-fold
What he had ſtolen away.

Thy payment ſhall but double be:
O then with speed reſign
My own seduced heart to me,
Accompanied with thine.

SIR WILLIAM DAVENANT.

SONG.

[1666?]

THE *lark now leaves his watery neſt,*
And climbing ſhakes his dewy wings;
He takes this window for the Eaſt,
And to implore your light he ſings.
Awake, awake, the morn will never rise
Till ſhe can dress her beauty at your eyes.

The merchant bows unto the seaman's ſtar,
The ploughman from the sun his season takes;
But ſtill the lover wonders what they are,
Who look for day before his miſtress wakes.
Awake, awake, break through your veils of lawn,
Then draw your curtains, and begin the dawn.

SIR WILLIAM DAVENANT.

TO CHLORIS.

[1670?]

FAREWELL, my sweet, until I come,
Improved in merit, for thy sake,
With characters of honour home,
Such as thou canſt not then but take.

To loyalty my love muſt bow,
My honour too calls to the field,
Where, for a lady's buſk, I now
Muſt keen and ſturdy iron wield.

Yet, when I ruſh into those arms,
Where death and danger do combine,
I ſhall less subject be to harms,
Than to those killing eyes of thine.

Since I could live in thy disdain,
Thou art so far become my Fate,
That I by nothing can be ſlain,
Until thy sentence speaks my date.

But if I seem to fall in war,
T' excuse the murder you commit,
Be to my memory just, so far
As in thy heart t' acknowledge it.

That's all I ask; which thou must give
To him, that, dying, takes a pride
It is for thee, and would not live,
Sole Prince of all the world beside.

CHARLES COTTON.

SONG.

[1670?]

I.

PHILLIS, men say that all my vows
Are to thy fortune paid;
Alas! my heart he little knows
Who thinks my love a trade.

II.

Were I of all these woods the lord,
One berry from thy hand
More real pleasure would afford
Than all my large command.

III.

My humble love has learned to live
On what the nicest maid,
Without a conscious blush, may give
Beneath the myrtle-shade.

SIR CHARLES SEDLEY.

SONG.

[1670?]

Not, Celia, that I juſter am,
Or better than the reſt,
For I would change each hour like them,
Were not my heart at reſt.

But I am tied to very thee,
By every thought I have;
Thy face I only care to see,
Thy heart I only crave.

All that in woman is adored
In thy dear self I find;
For the whole sex can but afford
The handsome, and the kind.

Why then ſhould I seek farther ſtore,
And ſtill make love anew?
When change itself can give no more,
'Tis easy to be true.

Sir Charles Sedley.

OUT OF LYCOPHRON.

[1670?]

What ſhall become of Man so wise,
When he dies?
None can tell
Whether he goes to Heaven or Hell:

Or, after a few moments dear,
He disappear,
And at last
Perish entirely like a beast.
But women, wine, and mirth, we know,
Are all the joys he has below;
Then let us ply those joys we have,
'Tis vain to think beyond the grave.
Out of our reach the gods have laid
Of time to come the event,
And laugh to see the fools afraid
Of what the knaves invent.

SIR CHARLES SEDLEY.

SONG.

[1671.]

I.

COME, *Chloris, hie we to the bower,*
To sport us ere the day be done:
Such is thy power that every flower
Will ope to thee as to the sun.

II.

And if a flower but chance to die
With my sighs' blast, or mine eyes' rain,
Thou canst revive it with thine eye,
And with thy breath make sweet again.

III.

The wanton suckling, and the vine,
Will ſtrive for th' honour, who firſt may
With their green arms encircle thine,
To keep the burning sun away.

THE ACADEMY OF COMPLIMENTS.

LOVE'S BRAVO.

[1674.]

WHY ſhould we murmur, why repine,
Phyllis, at thy fate, or mine?
Like prisoners, why do we these fetters ſhake,
Which neither thou, nor I, can break?
There is a better way to baffle Fate,
If mortals would but mind it,
And 'tis not hard to find it:
Who would be happy, muſt be desperate.
He muſt despise those ſtars that fright
Only fools that dread the night;
Time and Chance he muſt out-brave;
He that crouches is their ſlave.
Thus the wise Pagans, ill at ease,
Bravely chaſtised their surly Deities.

THOMAS FLATMAN.

SONG.

[1675.]

Cupid, I scorn to beg the art
From thy imaginary throne,
To learn to wound another's heart,
Or how to heal my own.

If ſhe be coy, my airy mind
Brooks not a ſiege; if ſhe be kind,
She proves my scorn that was my wonder;
For towns that yield I hate to plunder.

Love is a game; hearts are the prize;
Pride keeps the ſtakes, art throws the dice;
When either's won,
The game is done.
Love is a coward, hunts the flying prey,
But when it once ſtands ſtill, Love runs away.

Sir Francis Fane.

UNCERTAIN LOVE.

[1676.]

The labouring man that plants and sows,
His certain times of profit knows;
Seamen the rougheſt tempeſt scorn,
Hoping at laſt a rich return.
But my too much loved Celia's mind
Is more inconſtant and unkind
Than ſtormy weather, sea, or wind.

Now with assured hope raised high,
I think no man so blest as I;
Hope, that a dying saint may own,
To see and hear her speak alone.
What if I snatch one kiss, or more?
Where Heaven gives a wealthy store,
'Tis to be bounteous to the poor.

But ere my swiftest thought can thence
Convey a blessing to my sense,
My hope like fairy treasure's gone,
Although I never made it known.
From all untruth my heart is clean,
No other love can enter in;
Yet Celia's ne'er will come agen.

THOMAS DUFFÉTT.

THE MOWER TO THE GLOW-WORMS.

[1677?]

YE living lamps, by whose dear light
The nightingale does sit so late,
And studying all the summer night,
Her matchless songs does meditate;

Ye country comets, that portend
No war nor prince's funeral,
Shining unto no other end
Than to presage the grass's fall;

Ye glow-worms, whose officious flame
To wandering mowers shows the way,
That in the night have lost their aim,
And after foolish fires do stray:

Your courteous lights in vain ye waste,
Since Juliana here is come;
For she my mind hath so displaced,
That I shall never find my home.

ANDREW MARVELL.

LOVE AND LIFE.

[1678?]

ALL my past life is mine no more,
The flying hours are gone;
Like transitory dreams given o'er,
Whose images are kept in store
By Memory alone.

The time that is to come is not,
How can it then be mine?
The present moment's all my lot;
And that, as fast as it is got,
Phyllis, is only thine.

Then talk not of inconstancy,
False hearts, and broken vows;
If I, by miracle, can be
This livelong minute true to thee,
'Tis all that Heaven allows.

JOHN WILMOT, *Earl of Rochester.*

SONG.

[1680?]

FROM all uneasy passions free,
Revenge, ambition, jealousy,
Contented I had been too blest,
If Love and you had let me rest.
Yet that dull life I now despise;
Safe from your eyes
I feared no griefs, but then I found no joys.

Amidst a thousand kind desires,
Which beauty moves and love inspires,
Such pangs I feel of tender fear,
No heart so soft as mine can bear.
Yet I'll defy the worst of harms;
Such are your charms,
'Tis worth a life to die within your arms.

JOHN SHEFFIELD, *Duke of Buckingham.*

SONG.

[1696.]

CELIA is cruel; Sylvia, thou,
I must confess, art kind;
But in her cruelty, I vow,
I more repose can find.
For O, thy fancy at all games does fly,
Fond of address, and willing to comply.

Thus he that loves muſt be undone,
Each way on rocks we fall;
Either you will be kind to none,
Or, worse, be kind to all.
Vain are our hopes, and endless is our care:
We muſt be jealous, or we muſt despair.

Robert Gould.

AN INCANTATION.

[1696.]

I.

Choose the darkeſt part o' th' grove,
Such as ghoſts at noonday love.
Dig a trench, and dig it nigh
Where the bones of Laius lie;
Altars raised of turf, or ſtone,
Will the infernal powers have none.
Answer me, if this be done?
'Tis done.

II.

Is the sacrifice made fit?
Draw her backward to the pit:
Draw the barren heifer back:
Barren let her be, and black.
Cut the curled hair that grows
Full betwixt her horns and brows:
And turn your faces from the sun.
Answer me, if this be done?
'Tis done.

III.

Pour in blood, and blood-like wine,
To Mother Earth and Proserpine:
Mingle milk into the ſtream;
Feaſt the ghoſts that love the ſteam:
Snatch a brand from funeral pile:
Toss it in, to make them boil;
And turn your faces from the sun.
Answer me, if this be done?
'Tis done.

John Dryden.

ODE ON SOLITUDE.

[1702.]

Happy the man whose wiſh and care
A few paternal acres bound;
Content to breathe his native air
In his own ground.

Whose herds with milk, whose fields with bread,
Whose flocks supply him with attire:
Whose trees in summer yield him ſhade,
In winter fire.

Bleſſed who can unconcernedly find
Hours, days, and years, ſlide soft away,
In health of body, peace of mind,
Quiet by day;

Sound ſleep by night; ſtudy and ease
Together mixed; sweet recreation:
And innocence, which moſt does please,
With meditation.

Thus let me live, unseen, unknown,
Thus unlamented let me die:
Steal from the world, and not a ſtone
Mark where I lie.

ALEXANDER POPE.

SONG.

[1706.]

IF wine and muſic have the power
To ease the ſickness of the soul,
Let Phœbus every ſtring explore,
And Bacchus fill the sprightly bowl.
Let them their friendly aid employ,
To make my Chloe's absence light;
And seek for pleasure, to deſtroy
The sorrows of this livelong night.

But ſhe to-morrow will return;
Venus, be thou to-morrow great;
Thy myrtles ſtrow, thy odours burn,
And meet thy favourite nymph in ſtate.
Kind goddess, to no other powers
Let us to-morrow's bleſſings own;
Thy darling loves ſhall guide the hours,
And all the day be thine alone.

MATHEW PRIOR.

DIRGE IN CYMBELINE.

[1747.]

To fair Fidele's graſſy tomb
Soft maids and village hinds ſhall bring
Each opening ſweet of earlieſt bloom,
And rifle all the breathing Spring.

No wailing ghoſt ſhall dare appear,
To vex with ſhrieks this hallowed grove;
But ſhepherd lads aſſemble here,
And melting virgins own their love.

No withered witch ſhall here be seen;
No goblins lead their nightly crew:
The female fays ſhall haunt the green,
And dress thy grave with pearly dew.

The redbreaſt oft, at evening hours,
Shall kindly lend his little aid,
With hoary moss, and gathered flowers,
To deck the ground where thou art laid.

When howling winds, and beating rain,
In tempeſts ſhake the sylvan cell;
Or, midſt the chase, on every plain,
The tender thought on thee ſhall dwell;

Each lonely scene ſhall thee reſtore;
For thee the tear be duly ſhed;
Beloved till life can charm no more,
And mourned till Pity's self be dead!

William Collins.

A BACCHANALIAN

[1769?]

WHAT is war and all its joys?
Useless mischief, empty noise.
What are arms and trophies won?
Spangles glittering in the sun.
Rosy Bacchus, give me wine,
Happiness is only thine!

What is love without the bowl?
'Tis a languor of the soul:
Crowned with ivy, Venus charms,
Ivy courts me to her arms.
Bacchus, give me love and wine,
Happiness is only thine!

THOMAS CHATTERTON.

A RED, RED ROSE.

[1794.]

O MY luve's like a red, red rose,
That's newly sprung in June;
O my luve's like the melodie,
That's sweetly played in tune.

As fair art thou, my bonnie lass,
So deep in luve am I;
And I will luve thee ſtill, my dear,
Till a' the seas gang dry.

Till a' the seas gang dry, my dear,
And the rocks melt wi' the sun,
I will luve thee ſtill, my dear,
While the sands o' life ſhall run.

And fare thee weel, my only luve,
And fare thee weel awhile;
And I will come again, my luve,
Though it were ten thousand mile!

ROBERT BURNS.

SONG.

[1797.]

HEAR, sweet spirit, hear the spell,
Leſt a blacker charm compel!
So ſhall the midnight breezes swell
With thy deep long-lingering knell.

And at evening evermore,
In a chapel on the ſhore,
Shall the chanter, sad and saintly,
Yellow tapers burning faintly,
Doleful maſſes chant for thee,
Miserere Domine!

Hark! the cadence dies away
On the quiet moonlight sea:
The boatmen reſt their oars and say,
Miserere Domine!

SAMUEL TAYLOR COLERIDGE.

CHORAL SONG.

[1817.]

Up, up! ye dames, ye lasses gay!
To the meadows trip away.
'Tis you must tend the flocks this morn,
And scare the small birds from the corn.
Not a soul at home may stay:
For the shepherds must go
With lance and bow
To hunt the wolf in the woods to-day.

Leave the hearth and leave the house
To the cricket and the mouse:
Find grannam out a sunny seat,
With babe and lambkin at her feet.
Not a soul at home may stay:
For the shepherds must go
With lance and bow
To hunt the wolf in the woods to-day.

Samuel Taylor Coleridge.

SONG.

[1806?]

There's not a look, a word of thine,
My soul hath e'er forgot;
Thou ne'er hast bid a ringlet shine,
Nor given thy locks one graceful twine,
Which I remember not.

There never yet a murmur fell
From that beguiling tongue,
Which did not, with a lingering swell,
Upon my charmed senses dwell,
Like songs from Eden sung.

Ah, that I could, at once, forget
All, all that haunts me so;
And yet, thou witching girl, and yet,
To die were sweeter than to let
Thy loved remembrance go.

No; if this flighted heart muſt see
Its faithful pulse decay,
O let it die, remembering thee,
And, like the burnt aroma, be
Consumed in sweets away!

THOMAS MOORE.

[1806.]

O NIGHTINGALE! thou surely art
A creature of a "fiery heart:"
These notes of thine, they pierce and pierce:
Tumultuous harmony and fierce!
Thou ſing'ſt as if the God of wine
Had helped thee to a Valentine;
A song in mockery and despite
Of ſhades, and dews, and ſilent night;
And ſteady bliss, and all the loves
Now ſleeping in these peaceful groves.

I heard a Stock-dove sing or say
His homely tale, this very day;
His voice was buried among trees,
Yet to be come at by the breeze:
He did not cease; but cooed, and cooed;
And somewhat pensively he wooed:
He sang of love, with quiet blending,
Slow to begin, and never ending;
Of serious faith, and inward glee;
That was the song,—the song for me!

William Wordsworth.

TO THE LADY ANNE HAMILTON.

[1811.]

Too late I stayed—forgive the crime,
Unheeded flew the hours;
How noiseless falls the foot of Time,
That only treads on flowers!

What eye with clear account remarks
The ebbing of his glass,
When all its sands are diamond-sparks,
That dazzle as they pass?

Ah, who to sober measurement
Time's happy swiftness brings,
When birds of Paradise have lent
Their plumage for his wings?

Hon. William Robert Spencer.

SONG

[1814.]

YOUNG men will love thee more fair and more faſt;
Heard ye so merry the little bird ſing?
Old men's love the longeſt will laſt,
And the throſtle-cock's head is under his wing.

The young man's wrath is like light ſtraw on fire;
Heard ye so merry the little bird ſing?
But like red-hot ſteel is the old man's ire,
And the throſtle-cock's head is under his wing.

The young man will brawl at the evening board;
Heard ye so merry the little bird ſing?
But the old man will draw at the dawning the sword,
And the throſtle-cock's head is under his wing.

SIR WALTER SCOTT.

[1815.]

WASTED, weary, wherefore ſtay,
Wreſtling thus with earth and clay?
From the body pass away;
Hark! the mass is singing.

From thee doff thy mortal weed,
Mary Mother be thy speed,
Saints to help thee at thy need;
Hark! the knell is ringing.

Fear not snow-drift driving faſt,
Sleet, or hail, or levin blaſt;
Soon the ſhroud ſhall lap thee faſt,
And the ſleep be on thee caſt
That ſhall ne'er know waking.

Haſte thee, haſte thee, to be gone,
Earth flits faſt, and time draws on;
Gasp thy gasp, and groan thy groan,
Day is near the breaking.

SIR WALTER SCOTT.

SHE WALKS IN BEAUTY.

[1814.]

I.

SHE walks in beauty, like the night
Of cloudless climes and ſtarry ſkies;
And all that's beſt of dark and bright
Meet in her aspect and her eyes:
Thus mellowed to that tender light
Which heaven to gaudy day denies.

II.

One ſhade the more, one ray the less,
Had half impaired the nameless grace,
Which waves in every raven tress
Or softly lightens o'er her face;
When thoughts serenely sweet express
How pure, how dear their dwelling-place!

III.

And on that cheek, and o'er that brow,
So soft, so calm, yet eloquent,
The smiles that win, the tints that glow,
But tell of days in goodness spent,
A mind at peace with all below,
A heart whose love is innocent!

LORD BYRON.

SONG.

[1817.]

THINK not of it, sweet one, so,
Give it not a tear;
Sigh thou mayst, and bid it go
Any—anywhere.

Do not look so sad, sweet one,
Sad and fadingly;
Shed one drop (and only one),
O, 'twas born to die!

Still so pale? then, dearest, weep,
Weep,—I'll count the tears;
For each I will invent a bliss
For thee in after years.

Brighter has it left thine eyes
Than a sunny rill;
And thy whispering melodies
Are more tender still.

Yet, as all things mourn awhile
At fleeting blisses,
Let us too; but be our dirge
A dirge of kisses.

JOHN KEATS.

A FRAGMENT.

[1818.]

HENCE *Burgundy, Claret, and Port,*
Away with old Hock and Madeira;
Too earthly are ye for my sport;
Here's a beverage brighter and clearer.
Instead of a pitiful rummer,
My wine overbrims a whole Summer:
My bowl is the sky,
And I drink at my eye,
Till I feel in the brain
A Delphian pain,
Then follow, my Caius, then follow;
On the green of the hill
We will drink our fill
Of golden sunshine
Till our brains intertwine
With the glory and grace of Apollo!

JOHN KEATS.

SONG

[1819.]

FALSE friend, wilt thou smile, or weep,
When my life is laid asleep?
Little cares for a smile or a tear
The clay-cold corpse upon the bier;
Farewell! Heigh ho!
What is this whispers low?
There is a snake in thy smile, my dear,
And bitter poison within thy tear.

Sweet Sleep! were death like to thee,
Or if thou couldst mortal be,
I would close these eyes of pain;
When to wake? Never again.
O World! farewell!
Listen to the passing-bell!
It says, thou and I must part,
With a light and a heavy heart.

PERCY BYSSHE SHELLEY.

LOVE'S PHILOSOPHY.

[1820.]

I.

THE fountains mingle with the river,
And the rivers with the ocean;
The winds of heaven mix forever
With a sweet emotion:

Nothing in the world is ſingle;
All things by a law divine
In one another's being mingle—
Why not I with thine?

II.

See the mountains kiss high heaven,
And the waves clasp one another;
No ſiſter flower would be forgiven,
If it disdained its brother:
And the sunlight clasps the earth,
And the moonbeams kiss the sea:
What are all these kiſſings worth,
If thou kiss not me?

PERCY BYSSHE SHELLEY.

SONG.

[1821.]

RARELY, rarely, comeſt thou,
Spirit of Delight!
Wherefore haſt thou left me now
Many a day and night?
Many a weary night and day
'Tis ſince thou art fled away.

How ſhall ever one like me
Win thee back again?
With the joyous and the free
Thou wilt scoff at pain.

Spirit false! thou haſt forgot
All but those who need thee not.

As a lizard with the ſhade
Of a trembling leaf,
Thou with sorrow art dismayed;
Even the ſighs of grief
Reproach thee, that thou art not near,
And reproach thou wilt not hear.

Let me set my mournful ditty
To a merry measure;
Thou wilt never come for pity,
Thou wilt come for pleasure:
Pity then will cut away
Those cruel wings, and thou wilt ſtay.

I love all that thou loveſt,
Spirit of Delight!
The freſh Earth in new leaves dreſt,
And the ſtarry night;
Autumn evening, and the morn
When the golden miſts are born.

I love snow, and all the forms
Of the radiant froſt;
I love waves, and winds, and ſtorms,
Every thing almoſt
Which is Nature's, and may be
Untainted by man's misery.

I love tranquil solitude,
And such society
As is quiet, wise, and good;
Between thee and me
What difference? but thou dost possess
The things I seek, not love them less.

I love Love—though he has wings,
And like light can flee;
But, above all other things,
Spirit, I love thee:
Thou art love and life! O come,
Make once more my heart thy home.

PERCY BYSSHE SHELLEY.

◆

SONG TO MAY.

[1820?]

MAY! Queen of blossoms,
And fulfilling flowers,
With what pretty music
Shall we charm the hours?
Wilt thou have pipe and reed
Blown in the open mead?
Or to the lute give heed
In the green bowers?

Thou hast no need of us,
Or pipe or wire,
That hast the golden bee
Ripened with fire:

And many thousand more
Songſters, that thee adore,
Filling Earth's graſſy floor
With new deſire.

Thou haſt thy mighty herds,
Tame, and free livers;
Doubt not, thy muſic too
In the deep rivers:
And the whole plumy flight
Warbling the day and night—
Up at the gates of light,
See, the lark quivers!

When with the jacinth
Coy fountains are treſſed;
And for the mournful bird
Green-woods are dreſſed,
That did for Tereus pine;
Then ſhall our songs be thine,
To whom our hearts incline:
May, be thou bleſſed!

LORD THURLOW.

SONG TO THE EVENING STAR.

[1822.]

I.

STAR that bringeſt home the bee,
And sett'ſt the weary labourer free!
If any ſtar ſhed peace, 'tis thou,
That send'ſt it from above,

Appearing when Heaven's breath and brow
Are sweet as hers we love.

II.

Come to the luxuriant ſkies,
Whilſt the landscape's odours rise,
Whilſt far-off lowing herds are heard,
And songs when toil is done,
From cottages whose smoke unſtirred
Curls yellow in the sun.

III.

Star of love's soft interviews,
Parted lovers on thee muse;
Their remembrancer in Heaven
Of thrilling vows thou art,
Too delicious to be riven
By absence from the heart.

THOMAS CAMPBELL.

SONG.

[1825.]

I.

THE swallow leaves her neſt,
The soul my weary breaſt;
But therefore let the rain
On my grave
Fall pure; for why complain?
Since both will come again
O'er the wave.

II.

The wind dead leaves and snow
Doth hurry to and fro;
And, once, a day ſhall break
O'er the wave,
When a ſtorm of ghoſts ſhall ſhake
The dead, until they wake
In the grave.

THOMAS LOVELL BEDDOES.

DIRGE.

[1825.]

If thou wilt ease thy heart
Of love and all its smart,
Then ſleep, dear, ſleep;
And not a sorrow
Hang any tear on your eyelaſhes;
Lie ſtill and deep,
Sad soul, until the sea-wave waſhes
The rim o' the sun to-morrow,
In eaſtern ſky.

But wilt thou cure thy heart
Of love and all its smart?
Then die, dear, die;
'Tis deeper, sweeter,
Than on a rose-bank to lie dreaming
With folded eye;
And then alone, amid the beaming
Of love's ſtars, thou'lt meet her
In eaſtern ſky.

THOMAS LOVELL BEDDOES.

A SONG.

[1825.]

A CYPRESS-BOUGH, *and a rose-wreath sweet,*
A wedding-robe, and a winding-sheet,
A bridal-bed and a bier.
Thine be the kisses, maid,
And smiling Love's alarms;
And thou, pale youth, be laid
In the grave's cold arms.
Each in his own charms,
Death and Hymen both are here;
So up with scythe and torch,
And to the old church porch,
While all the bells ring clear:
And rosy, rosy the bed shall bloom,
And earthy, earthy heap up the tomb.

Now tremble dimples on your cheek,
Sweet be your lips to taste and speak,
For he who kisses is near:
By her the bride-god fair,
In youthful power and force;
By him the grizard bare,
Pale knight on a pale horse,
To woo him to a corpse.
Death and Hymen both are here;
So up with scythe and torch,
And to the old church porch,
While all the bells ring clear:
And rosy, rosy the bed shall bloom,
And earthy, earthy heap up the tomb.

THOMAS LOVELL BEDDOES.

BALLAD.

[1826?]

SPRING it is cheery,
Winter is dreary,
Green leaves hang, but the brown must fly;
When he's forsaken,
Withered and shaken,
What can an old man do but die?

Love will not clip him,
Maids will not lip him,
Maud and Marian pass him by;
Youth it is sunny,
Age has no honey:
What can an old man do but die?

June it was jolly,
O for its folly!
A dancing leg and a laughing eye;
Youth may be silly,
Wisdom is chilly:
What can an old man do but die?

Friends they are scanty,
Beggars are plenty,
If he has followers, I know why;
Gold's in his clutches,
(Buying him crutches!)
What can an old man do but die?

THOMAS HOOD.

BALLAD.

[1826?]

It was not in the winter
Our loving lot was cast:
It was the time of roses—
We plucked them as we passed!

That churlish season never frowned
On early lovers yet:
O, no—the world was newly crowned
With flowers when we met.

'Twas twilight, and I bade you go,
But still you held me fast;
It was the time of roses—
We plucked them as we passed!

THOMAS HOOD.

NEPHON'S SONG.

[1827.]

Lady and gentlemen fays, come buy!
No peddler has such a rich packet as I.

Who wants a gown
Of purple fold,
Embroidered down
The seams with gold?
See here!—a Tulip richly laced
To please a royal fairy's taste!

Who wants a cap
Of crimson grand?
By great good hap
I've one on hand:
Look, sir!—a Cock's-comb, flowering red,
'Tis juſt the thing, sir, for your head!

Who wants a frock
Of veſtal hue?
Or snowy smock?
Fair maid, do you?
O me!—a Lady smock so white!
Your bosom's self is not more bright!

Who wants to sport
A ſlender limb?
I've every sort
Of hose for him:
Both scarlet, ſtriped, and yellow ones:
The Woodbine makes such pantaloons!

Who wants—(huſh! huſh!)
A box of paint?
'Twill give a bluſh,
Yet leave no taint:
This Rose with natural rouge is filled,
From its own dewy leaves diſtilled.

Then lady and gentlemen fays, come buy!
You never will meet such a merchant as I.

George Darley.

A SERENADE.

[1827.]

I.

AWAKE thee, my Lady-love!
Wake thee, and rise!
The sun through the bower peeps
Into thine eyes!

II.

Behold how the early lark
Springs from the corn!
Hark, hark how the flower-bird
Winds her wee horn!

III.

The swallow's glad shriek is heard
All through the air!
The stock-dove is murmuring
Loud as she dare!

IV.

Apollo's winged bugleman
Cannot contain,
But peals his loud trumpet-call
Once and again!

V.

Then wake thee, my Lady-love!
Bird of my bower!
The sweetest and sleepiest
Bird at this hour!

GEORGE DARLEY.

[1830?]

I.

SWEET in her green dell the flower of beauty slumbers,
Lulled by the faint breezes sighing through her hair;
Sleeps she, and hears not the melancholy numbers
Breathed to my sad lute amid the lonely air!

II.

Down from the high cliffs the rivulet is teeming,
To wind round the willow-banks that lure him from above;
O that, in tears from my rocky prison streaming,
I, too, could glide to the bower of my love!

III.

Ah, when the woodbines with sleepy arms have wound her,
Opes she her eyelids at the dream of my lay,
Listening, like the dove, while the fountains echo round her,
To her lost mate's call in the forests far away!

IV.

Come, then, my bird! for the peace thou ever bearest,
Still Heaven's messenger of comfort to me;
Come! this fond bosom, my faithfullest, my fairest,
Bleeds with its death-wound—but deeper yet for thee!

GEORGE DARLEY.

THE CAVALIER'S SONG.

[1827.]

A STEED! *a steed of matchlesse speede!*
A sword of metal keene!
Al else to noble heartes is drosse,
Al else on earth is meane.
The neighynge of the war-horse prowde,
The rowleinge of the drum,
The clangour of the trumpet lowde,
Be soundes from heaven that come.
And, O! the thundering presse of knightes,
Whenas their war-cryes swelle,
May tole from heaven an angel bright,
And rowse a fiend from hell.

Then mounte! then mounte, brave Gallants all,
And don your helmes amaine;
Deathe's couriers, Fame and Honour, call
Us to the field againe.
No shrewish tears shal fill our eye,
When the sword-hilt's in our hand;
Heart-whole we'll parte, and no whit sighe
For the fayrest of the land.
Let piping swaine, and craven wight,
Thus weepe and puling crye;
Our businesse is like men to fighte,
And, like to Heroes, die!

WILLIAM MOTHERWELL.

SONG.

[1833.]

She is not fair to outward view,
As many maidens be;
Her loveliness I never knew
Until she smiled on me:
O, then I saw her eye was bright,
A well of love, a spring of light.

But now her looks are coy and cold,
To mine they ne'er reply;
And yet I cease not to behold
The love-light in her eye:
Her very frowns are better far
Than smiles of other maidens are!

Hartley Coleridge.

SONG.

[1834.]

Down lay in a nook my lady's brach,
And said, My feet are sore,
I cannot follow with the pack
A-hunting of the boar.

And though the horn sounds never so clear,
With the hounds in loud uproar,
Yet I must stop and lie down here,
Because my feet are sore.

The huntsman when he heard the same,
What answer did he give?
The dog that's lame is much to blame,
He is not fit to live.

HENRY TAYLOR.

THE BLACKBIRD.

[1835.]

MORNING.

GOLDEN bill! Golden bill!
Lo, the peep of day;
All the air is cool and ſtill,
From the elm-tree on the hill
Chant away:
While the moon drops down the weſt,
Like thy mate upon her neſt,
And the ſtars before the sun,
Melt like snow-flakes, one by one:
Let thy loud and welcome lay
Pour along
Few notes but ſtrong.

EVENING.

Jet-bright wing! Jet-bright wing!
Flit across the sunset glade;
Lying there in wait to ſing,
Liſten with thy head awry,
Keeping time with twinkling eye,
While from all the woodland ſhade

Birds of every plume and note
Strain the throat,
Till both hill and valley ring,
And the warbled minſtrelsy,
Ebbing, flowing like the sea,
Claims brief interludes from thee:
Then, with ſimple swell and fall,
Breaking beautiful through all,
Let thy Pan-like pipe repeat
Few notes but sweet.

JAMES MONTGOMERY.

A PHANTASY.

[1836.]

FEED *her with the leaves of Love,*
(Love, the rose, that bloſſoms here!)
Muſic, gently round her move!
Bind her to the cypress near!
Weave her round and round,
With ſkeins of ſilken sound!
'Tis a little ſtricken deer,
Who doth from the hunter fly,
And comes here to droop,—to die,
Ignorant of her wound!

Soothe her with sad ſtories,
O poet, till ſhe ſleep!
Dream's, come forth with all your glories!
Night, breathe soft and deep!

Music, round her creep!
If she steal away to weep,
Seek her out,—and, when you find her,
Gentle, gentlest Music, wind her
Round and round,
Round and round,
With your bands of softest sound:
Such as we, at nightfall, hear
In the wizard forest near,
When the charmed Maiden sings
At the wizard springs!

BRYAN WALLER PROCTER.

THE FAREWELL OF THE SOLDIER.

[1836.]

I LOVE *thee, I love thee,*
Far better than wine;
But the curse is above me,—
Thou'lt never be mine!

As the blade wears the scabbard,
The billow the shore,
So sorrow doth fret me
For evermore.

Fair beauty, I leave thee,
To conquer my heart:
I'll see thee, I'll bless thee,
And then—depart.

Let me take, ere I vaniſh,
One look of thine eyes,—
One smile for remembrance,
For life soon flies!

And now for the fortune
That hangeth above;
To bury, in battle,
My dream of love!

BRYAN WALLER PROCTER.

A BRIDAL DIRGE.

[1836.]

WEAVE no more the marriage chain!
All unmated is the lover;
Death has ta'en the place of Pain;
Love doth call on Love in vain:
Life and years of hope are over!

No more want of marriage bell!
No more need of bridal favour!
Where is ſhe to wear them well?
You, beſide the lover, tell!
Gone—with all the love he gave her!

Paler than the ſtone ſhe lies,
Colder than the winter's morning!
Wherefore did ſhe thus despise
(She with pity in her eyes)
Mother's care, and lover's warning?

Youth and beauty,—shall they not
Last beyond a brief to-morrow?
No: a prayer, and then forgot!
This the truest lover's lot;
This the sum of human sorrow!

BRYAN WALLER PROCTER.

A BACCHANALIAN SONG.

[1836.]

I.

SING!—Who sings
To her who weareth a hundred rings?
Ah, who is this lady fine?
The Vine, boys, the Vine!
The mother of mighty Wine.
A roamer is she
O'er wall and tree,
And sometimes very good company.

II.

Drink!—Who drinks
To her who blusheth and never thinks?
Ah, who is this maid of thine?
The Grape, boys, the Grape!
O, never let her escape
Until she be turned to Wine!
For better is she
Than Vine can be,
And very, very good company!

III.

Dream!—Who dreams
Of the God that governs a thousand streams?
Ah, who is this Spirit fine?
'Tis Wine, boys, 'tis Wine!
God Bacchus, a friend of mine.
O, better is he
Than grape or tree,
And the best of all good company!

BRYAN WALLER PROCTER.

SONG.

[1841.]

I.

YOU'LL love me yet! and I can tarry
Your love's protracted growing:
June reared that bunch of flowers you carry
From seeds of April's sowing.

II.

I plant a heartful now—some seed
At least is sure to strike
And yield—what you'll not pluck, indeed,
Not love, but, may be, like!

III.

You'll look at least on Love's remains,
A grave's one violet:
Your look? that pays a thousand pains.
What's death?—you'll love me yet!

ROBERT BROWNING.

SONG.

[1841.]

The year's at the Spring,
And day's at the morn;
Morning's at seven;
The hill-side's dew-pearled:
The lark's on the wing;
The snail's on the thorn;
God's in His heaven—
All's right with the world!

Robert Browning.

SONG.

[1842.]

The Moth's kiss, first!
Kiss me as if you made believe
You were not sure, this eve,
How my face, your flower, had pursed
Its petals up; so, here and there
You brush it, till I grow aware
Who wants me, and wide open burst.

The Bee's kiss, now!
Kiss me as if you entered gay
My heart at some noonday,
A bud that dares not disallow
The claim, so all is rendered up,
And passively its shattered cup
Over your head to sleep I bow.

Robert Browning.

THE LOST MISTRESS.

[1845.]

ALL's over, then—does truth sound bitter,
As one at firſt believes?
Hark, 'tis the sparrows' good-night twitter
About your cottage eaves!

And the leaf-buds on the vine are woolly,
I noticed that to-day;
One day more burſts them open fully
—You know the red turns gray.

To-morrow we meet the same then, deareſt?
May I take your hand in mine?
Mere friends are we,—well, friends the mereſt
Keep much that I'll reſign:

For each glance of that eye so bright and black,
Though I keep with heart's endeavour,—
Your voice, when you wiſh the snow-drops back,
Though it ſtays in my soul forever!

ROBERT BROWNING.

RONDEAU.

[1844.]

JENNY kiſſed me when we met,
Jumping from the chair ſhe sat in;
Time, you thief, who love to get
Sweets into your liſt, put that in:

Say I'm weary, say I'm sad,
Say that health and wealth have missed me,
Say I'm growing old, but add,
Jenny kissed me.

LEIGH HUNT.

CUPID SWALLOWED.

A PARAPHRASE FROM THE ANTHOLOGY.

[1844.]

T'OTHER day, as I was twining
Roses, for a crown to dine in,
What, of all things, midst the heap
Should I light on, fast asleep,
But the little desperate elf,
The tiny traitor, Love himself!
By the wings I pinched him up
Like a bee, and in a cup
Of my wine I plunged and sank him,
And what d'ye think I did?—I drank him.
Faith, I thought him dead. Not he!
There he lives with tenfold glee;
And now this moment with his wings
I feel him tickling my heart-strings.

LEIGH HUNT.

SONG.

[1846.]

ONE year ago my path was green,
My footstep light, my brow serene;
Alas! and could it have been so
One year ago?

There is a love that is to laſt
When the hot days of youth are paſt:
Such love did a sweet maid beſtow
One year ago.

I took a leaflet from her braid
And gave it to another maid.
Love! broken ſhould have been thy bow
One year ago.

WALTER SAVAGE LANDOR.

SONG.

[1846.]

I LOVE to hear that men are bound
By your enchanting links of sound:
I love to hear that none rebel
Againſt your beauty's ſilent spell.
I know not whether I may bear
To see it all, as well as hear;
And never ſhall I clearly know
Unless you nod and tell me so.

WALTER SAVAGE LANDOR.

SONG.

[1846.]

LITTLE it intereſts me how
Some insolent usurper now
Divides your narrow chair;

Little heed I whose hand is placed
(No, nor how far) around your waiſt,
Or paddles in your hair.

A time, a time there may have been
(Ah! and there was) when every scene
Was brightened by your eyes.
And dare you aſk what you have done?
My answer, take it, is but one—
The weak have taught the wise.

WALTER SAVAGE LANDOR.

SONG.

[1846.]

OFTEN *have I heard it said*
That her lips are ruby-red.
Little heed I what they say,
I have seen as red as they.
Ere ſhe smiled on other men,
Real rubies were they then.

When ſhe kiſſed me once in play,
Rubies were less bright than they,
And less bright were those which ſhone
In the palace of the Sun.
Will they be as bright again?
Not if kiſſed by other men.

WALTER SAVAGE LANDOR.

THE AGE OF WISDOM.

[1846.]

I.

Ho, pretty page, with the dimpled chin,
That never has known the barber's ſhear,
All your wiſh is woman to win,
This is the way that boys begin,—
Wait till you come to Forty Year.

II.

Curly gold locks cover fooliſh brains,
Billing and cooing is all your cheer;
Sighing and ſinging of midnight ſtrains,
Under Bonnybell's window-panes,—
Wait till you come to Forty Year!

III.

Forty times over let Michaelmas pass,
Grizzling hair the brain doth clear—
Then you know a boy is an ass,
Then you know the worth of a lass,
Once you have come to Forty Year.

IV.

Pledge me round, I bid ye declare,
All good fellows whose beards are gray,
Did not the faireſt of the fair
Common grow and wearisome ere
Ever a month was paſt away?

V.

The reddeſt lips that ever have kiſſed,
The brighteſt eyes that ever have ſhone,
May pray and whisper, and we not liſt,
Or look away, and never be miſſed,
Ere yet ever a month is gone.

VI.

Gillian's dead, GOD reſt her bier;
How I loved her twenty years syne!
Marian's married, but I ſit here
Alone and merry at Forty Year,
Dipping my nose in the Gascon wine.

WILLIAM MAKEPEACE THACKERAY.

SONG.

[1846.]

O, THAT we two were Maying
Down the ſtream of the soft Spring breeze;
Like children with violets playing
In the ſhade of the whispering trees.

O, that we two sat dreaming
On the sward of some ſheep-trimmed down,
Watching the white miſt ſteaming
Over river and mead and town.

O, that we two lay ſleeping
In our neſt in the churchyard sod,
With our limbs at reſt on the quiet Earth's breaſt,
And our souls at home with GOD!

CHARLES KINGSLEY.

SONG.

[1856]

THE world goes up, and the world goes down,
And the sunshine follows the rain:
And yesterday's sneer and yesterday's frown
Can never come over again,
Sweet wife,
No, never come over again.

For woman is warm though man be cold,
And the night will hallow the day;
Till the heart which at even was weary and old,
Can rise in the morning gay,
Sweet wife,
To its work in the morning gay.

CHARLES KINGSLEY.

[1848?]

THY voice is heard through rolling drums,
That beat to battle where he stands;
Thy face across his fancy comes,
And gives the battle to his hands:
A moment, while the trumpets blow,
He sees his brood about thy knee;
The next, like fire he meets the foe,
And strikes him dead for thine and thee.

ALFRED TENNYSON.

[1848?]

As through the land at eve we went,
And plucked the ripened ears,
We fell out, my wife and I,
O we fell out, I know not why,
And kissed again with tears.

For when we came where lies the child
We lost in other years,
There above the little grave,
O there above the little grave,
We kissed again with tears.

ALFRED TENNYSON.

[1848?]

SWEET and low, sweet and low,
Wind of the western sea,
Low, low, breathe and blow,
Wind of the western sea!
Over the rolling waters go,
Come from the dying moon, and blow,
Blow him again to me:
While my little one, while my pretty one, sleeps.

Sleep and rest, sleep and rest,
Father will come to thee soon;
Rest, rest, on mother's breast,
Father will come to thee soon;

Father will come to his babe in the neſt,
Silver sails all out of the west
Under the ſilver moon:
Sleep, my little one, ſleep, my pretty one, ſleep.

Alfred Tennyson.

[1850?]

Come not when I am dead,
To drop thy fooliſh tears upon my grave,
To trample round my fallen head,
And vex the unhappy duſt thou wouldſt not save.
There let the wind sweep, and the plover cry,
But thou, go by.

Child, if it were thine error or thy crime,
I care no longer, being all unbleſt:
Wed whom thou wilt, but I am ſick of Time,
And I deſire to reſt.
Pass on, weak heart, and leave me where I lie:
Go by, go by.

Alfred Tennyson.

THE SENTENCES.

[1856.]

Thais, my heart's no match for thine:
Waſte not thy warmth on me; but go
Seek out some chillier spirit; mine
Aſks not another fire, but snow.

The lack of lovely pride in her
Who ſtrives to please, my pleasure numbs;
And ſtill the maid I moſt prefer
Whose care to please with pleaſing comes.

COVENTRY PATMORE.

THE REVELATION.

[1856.]

An idle Poet, here and there,
Looks round him, but, for all the reſt,
The world, unfathomably fair,
Is duller than a witling's jeſt.
Love wakes men, once a lifetime each;
They lift their heavy lids, and look;
And lo, what one sweet page can teach
They read with joy, then ſhut the book:
And some give thanks, and some blaspheme,
And moſt forget; but, either way,
That and the Child's unheeded dream
Is all the light of all their day.

COVENTRY PATMORE.

INDEX OF WRITERS

AND

PUBLICATIONS.

Cowley, Abraham 1618–1667
Cox, Robert .... 17th Century
Crashaw, Richard .... 1615?–1650?

Daniel, Samuel 1562–1619
Darley, George 1785–1849
Davenant, Sir William 1605–1668
Davies, Sir John 1570–1626
Dekker, Thomas .... 15—–1639?
Denham, Sir John 1615–1668
Digges, Leonard 1588–1635
Donne, John 1573–1631
Drayton, Michael 1563–1631
Drummond, William 1585–1649
Dryden, John 1631–1700
Duffett, Thomas .... 17th Century

Etherege, Sir George .... 1636?–1694?

Fane, Sir Francis .... 17th Century
Fanshaw, Sir Richard 1607–1666
Field, Nathaniel .... 15—–1638?
Flatman, Thomas .... 1633?–1668
Flecknoe, Richard .... 17th Century
Fletcher, Giles .... 1588?–1623
Fletcher, John 1576–1625
Ford, John .... 1586–1640?
Ford, Thomas .... 17th Century

Glapthorne, Henry .... 17th Century
Goffe, Thomas 1592–1627
Gomersall, Robert 1600–1646
Gould, Robert .... 17th Century
Greene, Robert 1560–1592
Greville, Fulke, *Lord Brooke* 1554–1628

Habington, William 1605–1654
Harington, John 1534–1582
Herbert, George 1593–1632
Herrick, Robert 1591–1674
Heywood, Thomas .... 1580?-1649?
Hood, Thomas 1798–1845
Hookes, N. .... 17th Century
Howard, Sir Robert 1622–1698
Hughes, H. .... 17th Century
Hunt, Leigh 1784–1859

Jonson, Ben 1574–1637

Keats, John 1795–1821
Killigrew, Henry .... 1612–1688?
Kinaston, Sir Francis .... 15—1642?
King, Henry, *Bishop of Chichester* 1591–1669
Kingsley, Charles 1819–

Lluellin, Martin .... 17th Century
Lodge, Thomas 1556–1625
Lovekin, Philonax .... 17th Century
Lovelace, Richard 1618–1658
Lyly, John 1554–1600

Markham, Gervase .... 17th Century
Marlowe, Christopher 1562–1593
Marvell, Andrew 1620–1678
Massinger, Philip 1584–1640
May, Thomas 1595–1650
Milton, John 1608–1674
Montgomery, James 1771–1854
Moore, Thomas 1779–1852
Motherwell, William 1797–1835

Nabbes, Thomas .... 1612?–1645
Nash, Thomas .... 1564?–1601?

Patmore, Coventry 1823–
Peele, George .... 1552?–1597?
Pembroke, William Herbert, *Earl of* 1580–1630
Pope, Alexander 1688–1744
Prior, Mathew 1664–1721
Procter, Bryan Waller ("*Barry Cornwall*") 1787–

Raleigh, Sir Walter 1552–1618
Randolph, Thomas 1605–1634
Rochester, John Wilmot, *Earl of* 1647–1680
Rowley, Samuel .... 17th Century

Sampson, William .... 17th Century
Scott, Sir Walter 1771–1832
Sedley, Sir Charles 1639–1701
Shakespeare, William 1564–1616
Shelley, Percy Bysshe 1792–1822
Sherburne, Sir Edward 1618–1702
Shirley, James 1596–1666
Sidney, Sir Philip 1554–1586
Spencer, Hon. William Robert 1770–1834
Stanley, Thomas .... 1625?–1678
Suckling, Sir John .... 1608–1641?
Surrey, Henry Howard, *Earl of* 1517–1547

Taylor, Henry .... 19th Century
Tennyson, Alfred 1810–
Thackeray, William Makepeace 1811–1863
Thurlow, Edward, *Lord* .... 19th Century

Vaughan, Henry 1621–1695

WALLER, EDMUND 1605–1687
WALTON, IZAAK.................................... 1593–1683
WATSON, THOMAS 1560–1591
WEBSTER, JOHN.................................... 15—16—
WITHER, GEORGE.................................... 1588–1667
WORDSWORTH, WILLIAM 1770–1850
WOTTON, SIR HENRY 1568–1639
WYATT, SIR THOMAS 1503–1542

ACADEMY OF COMPLIMENTS.
ALLISON'S HOUR'S RECREATION IN MUSIC.
BATESON'S MADRIGALS.
BYRD'S SONGS.
DAVISON'S POETICAL RHAPSODY.
DOWLAND'S BOOK OF SONGS.
FARMER'S ENGLISH MADRIGALS.
MORLEY'S MADRIGALS.
MUSICA TRANSALPINA.
MYSTERIES OF LOVE AND ELOQUENCE.
PILKINGTON'S MADRIGALS.
SICILY AND NAPLES: A TRAGEDY.
WARD'S MADRIGALS.
WEELKES'S AIRS.
WEELKES'S BALLADS.
WEELKES'S MADRIGALS.
WILBYE'S MADRIGALS.
WIT'S RECREATIONS.

INDEX OF FIRST LINES.

PAGE

PAGE

THE END.

CPSIA information can be obtained
at www.ICGtesting.com
Printed in the USA
LVHW090312060122
707841LV00013B/91

9 783752 554007